Captives of the Troglodytes

A faint whimpering cry came to his ears. Twisting his head, Diodric saw that the Lady Niane was also captive, and was being half-dragged along in the clutches of grunting Troglodytes. He spat a curse from dry lips crusted with dust. It would have been better for her to have taken her own life than to have fallen alive into the hands of these vile and depraved little monstrosities. There were unutterable uses to which the grimy, chittering horde would put the body of a beautiful young woman.

But no torture or savagery would move the Lady Niane to surrender what she was sworn to guard until her last agonized breath—the treasure of the world. . . .

The Black Star

LIN CARTER

A DELL BOOK

Published by
Dell Publishing Co., Inc.
1 Dag Hammarskjold Plaza
New York, New York 10017

The Black Star

is dedicated to:

POUL ANDERSON,
FRANK PRICE,
and
LARRY SHAW

★ The Prologue to The Black Star ★

It is written:

> O, Solon, though many and mighty are the deeds recorded in our Sacred Writings, yet there is one which surpasses all the rest in magnitude and glory. For these histories relate of a time when the Atlantic Sea was navigable, and there was an Island before those straits which you call the Pillars of Hercules, an Island greater than Libya, from which you might pass to the other islands in the great Sea.
>
> Now in this Island of Atlantis, a combination of kings was formed, a great and wonderful Empire which, with mighty power subdued the whole Island, together with many

other islands, and besides they subjected to their dominion portions of the continent of Africa.

But in succeeding time, prodigious earthquakes and deluges occurred, and in a single night and a day the Island of Atlantis disappeared and was sunk beneath the Sea.

—PLATO: The *Timaeus,* 24.D

There lay in the deep off Libya, in the ocean beyond the Pillars of Hercules, an island of considerable size, distant from Libya a number of days' voyage to the west. It was a fruitful and mountainous island, with a level plain of surpassing beauty.

. . . The most civilized men among the inhabitants of those regions were the Atlantioi, who dwelt in a prosperous country and possessed great cities.

It was in this Island that mythology sets the Birthplace of the Immortal Gods.

—DIODORUS SICULUS: The *Library of History,* V.19

They became tall with pride. "We are the kings; we are the gods." They took wives. They bred monsters. They built temples to the human body.

Then the Third Eye worked no longer.

They built huge cities. Of rare earths and metals they built. Out of the white stone and the black stone they cut images and worshiped them.

They built great images nine *yatis* high.

Inner fires had destroyed the fland of their fathers. The waters threatened them, the Fourth race.

The first great waters came. They swallowed the seven islands.

All holy were saved; the unholy, destroyed.

—THE BOOK OF DZYAN: stanzas 40-46.

The Island of Atlantis, which was of great magnitude and of even greater power, as Plato records, in one day and night was overwhelmed beneath the sea. The priests and prophets of the Egyptians preserve a tradition that the gods visited this doom upon the Atlanteans because they had turned from the worship of heaven to worship themselves, their bodies, their kings. But I have heard that they also committed the sin of black magic, wherefor the anger of the gods was brought down upon them, and all their splendid cities were destroyed and their wisdom perished.

—PHILO JUDAEUS, xxvi, quoting from the lost *Meropis* of Theopompus

The Dhyanis were not always good. Their king, *Thevetata*, was one . . . It was under the evil influence of this King-Demon that the

Atlantis-race became a nation of wicked magicians.

—HELENA PETROVNA BLAVATSKY: *The Secret Doctrine,* Vol. II, p. 222

Here begins a tale of the Lost Continent, in the days before the Cataclysm, ere history was born.

★

The Black Star

The Book of Diodric

No longer submitting to the wise rule of the Initiate emperors, the followers of the Black Arts rose in rebellion and set up a rival emperor, who, after much struggle and fighting, drove the White Emperor from his capital, the City of the Golden Gates, and established himself on his throne.

—W. Scott-Elliot: *Atlantis and the Lost Lemuria* (edition of 1954, p. 29)

i. On the Parapet

Sunset flamed crimson in the west, and the City of
the Golden Gates, which was the sacred capital of
High Atlantis, lay ravaged and burning, half in
ruin, half deserted, all but helpless in the hand of
its evil conqueror.

A young warrior named Diodric leaned wearily
on the marble parapet of the imperial palace. He
was exhausted from the long endless fury of battle,
sick of blood, and near the limits of his endurance.
Tears stung his eyes as he gazed out over the splendid panorama of the City, as he saw the empty
palaces, the wreckage in the streets, the oily smoke
of burning temples. He leaned his brow against his
arms and felt the bitter tang of despair like brass on
his tongue. Everything that was high and noble
had perished from the world; only ugliness and the
long decline of the world stretched from this point

of time into the darkness of the future.

Because he was young and fierce-hearted and filled with impetuous hot emotion, he wept there as long shadows and the darkness of night gathered above the City like flocking vultures eager to feed on the corpses of the fallen. He wept as a child weeps: hoarse, gulping sobs racked his chest; shuddering tempests of emotion shook him from head to foot. The City was fallen . . . the Empire was ended . . . what use for him to hold onto life?

Should a Throne warrior outlive the Empire that had nurtured him?

The next wave of the onslaught would take the parapet and the half-deserted palace would be lost. This palace, the Great House, that was built on the most holy soil of all Atlantis, the Mount of Cleito at the heart of the City, would fall into the claws of the Dragon.

Why let some swarthy, snarling Dragon warrior take his life at spear point? The ancient heroes of the Atlanteans, when the hour of their death was upon them, had cut their warrior's braid with the little holy knife worn ever above the heart, had sung their Death Song, and had let the slim sacred blade drink of their heart's blood, and went down into the Kingdom of Darkness in the way of heroes.

With a swift impulsiveness, the boy Diodric snatched out the little *sax*-knife, kissed it, and snatched at his braided hair. The first verses of his Death Song were almost upon his lips. He was not even of the Atlantean race—his yellow braid and clear blue eyes and the fairness of his skin would have told you that he was a child of the primitive Celts, could you have seen him there on the marble parapet. But his ancestors, carried off as slaves by the Atlanteans from the coasts of Thuria, had earned their freedom, and the texture of his mind and character were as Atlantean as if he wore the olive skin and black hair and dark oblique eyes of a Turanian.

Though no Atlantean by race, he could at least die like one. Sunset flashed scarlet on the slim orichalcum blade as he lifted the holy knife to sever his braid. He would sing his Song and sheath the little blade in his bold young heart and go down into the Kingdom of Darkness to dwell with the heroes of olden time.

But the motion was arrested. Suddenly a quavering, weak voice from the gathering shadows said: "Don't do it, lad—don't throw your life away. *Live!*"

ii. The Old Warrior, Dying

Diodric turned to look at the old gray-headed veteran at the next station. All that day they had fought together side by side and he did not even know the man's name. The old warrior had taken a spear in the belly in the last wave, or the one before that. Diodric had assumed his unknown comrade was dead, slumped in the shadows of the wall. Now he turned, and almost absent-mindedly he slid the *sax*-knife into its sheath again and went to where the other lay.

He knelt down, took the water bottle from his belt, and set it against the old warrior's lips. The other drank thirstily for a time, then shoved the bottle aside with a weak hand.

"Save the rest for yourself, boy," he muttered. "I shall not thirst for long."

"Is it bad?" the boy asked soberly. The old man grunted.

"To the death." He looked up with keen, old eyes in a lean gaunt face to search the boy's visage. The eyes lost their keenness and glazed and wandered. "Has night fallen yet?"

"Not yet, but night is near."

The old man forced a weary laugh. " 'Not yet, but night is near,' " he repeated in a faint voice. He forced another laugh, and a trickle of red blood ran from the corner of his mouth to stain his beard. "Aye, night is near enough, boy . . . the Long Night itself, and no man living shall see the coming of the Dawn . . . Ah, well; I, at least, will not live to see Thelatha the Accursed squatting on the Throne of Atlantis. That's something to be grateful for."

He squinted up at Diodric's pale, grimy face through the purple gloom. "Live, boy. You are young, life burns fierce within you. Why throw away another life, into the pit where so many thousands have fallen? Live, wed, sire strong sons to fight for the glories we have lost this day . . . ah, God Pazadon . . . Father Pazadon . . . how *much* we have lost this day!"

Diodric lifted the old man's head upon his thigh and wet a corner of his scarf from the bottle to wipe the old man's face. He wiped away the stain of blood, but with every gasping breath that racked the other's bony frame, more scarlet spurted forth into the grizzled beard. The spear thrust had slanted into the old man's gut, but it must have missed his vital organs. It was loss of blood that had drained his strength to the brink of death. For he lay in a spreading scarlet pool and his long legs were beslimed with gore.

The old man mumbled, staring with glazed, unseeing eyes at nothing. His mind seemed to wander for a time. He muttered disjointedly of old wars and vanished glories and of kings long since gone down to dust, kings that were but names to the young Celt, battles already dim and distant, glories that the future would forget.

Diodric knelt there patiently, holding the dying warrior. There was nothing that he could do to ease the old man's passing; but no man should die all alone, and he knelt there to give what comfort his presence could give the dying warrior. At length the dying old man roused himself a little and squinted blearily up at Diodric's smoke-stained face.

"That last wave almost took us, boy," he wheezed, not seeming to notice the gory drops that dribbled into his beard with every breath he exhaled. Then he said, musingly, "They say the Emperor has already fled the City by a secret way."

Diodric nodded somberly. "So I have heard. Captain Ergon made his round of the battlements after the last assault. He said the Emperor was safe with the Sacred Family and would take refuge in one of the loyal cities of the west."

"Aye . . . aye . . . I have served him and his father, the Divine Metemphet, thirty years in this harness,"—his gnarled fingers plucked feebly at the steel breastplate he wore, stroking the Sun emblem worked thereon—"even as *my* father served *his* father, Amsham the Glorious, in days gone by. They say that the Empress is safe, too?"

Diodric nodded. "The Lord Pnomphis and the Royal Lady escaped together into the west; doubtless the Emperor will raise an army and return to take the City."

The old man cackled, then sighed. "Not in your time, boy, and not in mine. The Emperor will live and die in exile . . . and the Long Night cometh down over all this land . . . poor Lady! Her babe will be born beside some rough road, rather than in the God Chamber."

Diodric said nothing. It was known that the wife of Pnomphis the White Emperor was with child and near the time of her delivery. But now the old man's mind was wandering again.

"Thirty years . . . many battles, aye, and honors, too . . . the Lord Metemphet, you know, could name me at sight . . . 'I see Shemosh is in the ranks,' he would say, reviewing the Throne Legion before a battle, 'that means we shall have victory, my Lords!' I heard him say it, many the time."

Then the light went out of his eyes and his soul went down into the Kingdom of Darkness to dwell in the cold halls of the restless dead.

He had met death with a comrade at his side.

iii. "Flee, You Young Fool!"

Diodric washed the dead face clean with fresh water and a bit of rag, and laid the corpse out straight, closing the gnarled old hands over the hilt of his sword, which he set upon the dead man's chest. Then, wearily, he got to his feet and strode back to his post. Odd that the Dragons had not attacked the walls before this.

For seven long days and flaming nights the battle had raged about the City of the Golden Gates. Upon word of the approach of the Demon King and his host of savage Dragon warriors, the White Emperor had summoned his nephew, King Thion of Meropis, and the King of Kernê, and Zophtus, a third tributary king. They had come with all their hosts, but courage alone could not prevail before the withering blasts of magic Thelatha hurled up against them. The legions of three cities had gone down before the Dragon like ripe wheat before the scythe.

But the City itself held firm against Thelatha. The Throne Legion held it, and made the Dragon warriors pay dearly for every foot of space they were forced to yield up. Ring by ring, wall by wall, zone by zone, canal by canal, they were driven back. At last the Outer City had fallen before the magical weapon wherewith the Dragon warriors were armed: the Black Fire it was called, and it cast a weird dark flame that burned stone, metal, and flesh, and the fires thereof could not be extinguished with water. Indeed, to this hour, oily smoke rose from the wreckage of mansion, palace, temple, and forum in the City beyond, where uncanny flames yet smouldered: flame that was dark as any shadow, and threw off not heat but *cold*.

The clank of metal against stone, loud in the stillness of twilight which was broken only by the distant rustle of flames and faint cries from the deserted City, made Diodric turn, snatching up his great spear.

But it was only the captain, Ergon. Pale of face, his plumed helm gone, his cloak of Imperial scarlet in rags, the officer emerged from the gloom. His cold eyes took in the corpse of old Shemosh where Diodric had laid the body, and his pale face was suddenly drawn and bitter. There were weary lines about his eyes.

"Still here, lad?" he said in a clipped voice. "The cohort guarding the south parapet has gone down into the City, hoping to make Meropis Gate and escape before the City is invested in force."

"What of my cohort, lord?" asked the youth. The officer shrugged.

"Dead, most of 'em. The last wave all but took the wall; the next one will, for certain. You may as well try to save yourself."

Save yourself.

Diodric touched the hilt of the holy knife at his breast, remembering. Almost had he cut his braid, sung his Death Song. But the other man, the dying man, had saved him from the impulsive act his fierce, impetuous mood of the moment had almost begun. Now the moment was past, his mood had changed. Suddenly he wanted very much to live: the feel of the evening breeze against his sweating, grimy face was tonic; the young vigor in his loins, the young strength in his thews, cried out against extinction.

"I should rather stay and defend my—"

The captain laughed harshly, almost mockingly. "Defend what, boy? A deserted City—an empty palace? We have abandoned the City to the enemy; all have fled the Great House save a few slaves, a few looters!"

The officer's shoulders slumped. He looked suddenly very weary and his eyes went dull. "All is lost here. Go, boy, while you can. Perchance you can join the Emperor in the west. He will be raising troops against the Dragon. He will come back someday, to wrest the City from the conqueror. He can use that strong young arm of yours." He looked up, seeing the indecision in the boy's face. His cold bitter expression softened.

"You look like a lettered youth of decent family. Have you ever read Kemthon the philosopher? He has a counsel: 'Never can you be certain that your life may not someday be valuable to another.' Those are wise words."

There was thoughtful melancholy in the older man's voice; then despair and helpless fury twisted his mouth, and he raged savagely: *"Flee, you young fool! I have dead men enough on my conscience!"*

And he was gone. Diodric stood and watched the tall, spare figure as it receded down the parapet, steel greaves ringing at every step.

As he strode away, the captain held his back as stiff and straight as if he were on parade.

Watching the proud, lonely officer making his round of guard posts now deserted by fleeing men or held only by corpses, the boy felt that he watched the greatness of High Atlantis receding down dim vistas of time into the forgotten past.

iv. The Assassins

Some little while later a faint cry caught his attention. He looked and saw a running girl emerge from the thick gloom of the colonnade that rose from this level to support the parapet of the next tier of the mighty pyramidlike palace.

She was no kitchen drab, from her fine blue gown. Some woman of the court left behind when the Imperial party made hasty exodus from the doomed City of the Golden Gates. As she ran she hugged a bundle of clothing against her breast; perhaps she had lingered too long in completing some last duty or in gathering her possessions together, and had not been able to join the main body of courtiers when they fled. He wondered why she had cried out. She was too distant for him to see anything but the blue length of her gown and the pale blur of her face.

Then he saw the men that were on her heels.

There were two of them, dark figures, their faces hidden behind black cowls and scarves drawn up over their noses. They ran after her on silent feet, like hounds after a fleeing deer. And like hounds they caught up with her and dragged her down.

He left his great iron-shod spear where he had leaned it against the parapet, and ran across the open plaza of the tier, whipping his sword clear of its scabbard with a rasping of steel against leather. Blue eyes burning with wrath, he hurled himself to the defense of the helpless woman.

For a swift flashing moment the words of the old philosopher whom Captain Ergon had quoted returned to his thoughts. *Never can you be certain that your life may not someday be valuable to another*. Then thought vanished and fighting fury rose as he flung himself upon the masked men.

They had caught the woman and dragged her down, and one now stood astride her body, tearing at the bundle she clasped to her breast. Diodric assumed without conscious thought that they were looters and that their motive in seizing the lady was simple lust. Rape and plunder follow the fall of a city; they are natural consequences of conquest, but nonetheless despicable.

He seized one man by the shoulder and dragged him half around. He caught one flash of venomous glaring eyes above the black kerchief masking the rest of the man's face. He drove the sword into the man's belly and ripped it out—whirling to meet the attack of the second masked man, who had cried out a certain Name and flung himself upon Diodric with a long dagger clenched in one swarthy fist.

Diodric caught the blade on his steel cuirass, where it broke. His dripping sword swung, splattering the air with scarlet droplets, biting deep into the man's side. He coughed a gout of blood, sagged over and fell to the stone pavement and lay sprawled in the tangle of his cloak, like the black shadow cast by some ungainly and immense bird.

The young warrior stooped, wiping his blade clean on the bedraggled black cloak. Then he froze as the implications of the involuntary cry his attack had wrung from the lips of the first masked man came home to him. The Name of the Dark Power the legions of the Dragon worshiped was not unknown to him. It was not a Name to be spoken aloud. And Diodric recoiled from the sprawled corpse as a man draws back in loathing from a serpent in his path.

These were no looters, but spies of the enemy!

He turned to the fallen woman who lay sobbing for breath on the cold pavement. And when she lifted to him a young face, pale and exquisite, with soft, full lips warm and ripe, and when he looked into eyes that were gray, immense, luminous, and fringed with thick black lashes like dark shadows in her tear-stained face, he was suddenly glad he had not sung his Death Song yet.

v. Niane

"Are you hurt, mistress?" he asked. He knew her at a glance: the Lady Niane, one of the Queen's women. He had seen her at court many times, but always at a distance. She shook her head, and her great eyes slid from him to the obscene, sprawled corpses. She shuddered convulsively.

"No—not hurt," she gasped.

He bent and helped her to her feet, reaching for her bundle. She snatched her belongings from his hand, clasped them to her small young breasts, but let him assist her to rise.

"All this—death."

He nodded, his young face serious, and cleared his throat uncertainly. Diodric was not at his ease with women of high station: he could not make idle conversation easily, as did the glib young lordlings of the court. Not that he was in awe of her station, although hers was an ancient and noble House. He was himself sprung from a fine old House, one that had risen from slavery to nobility through distinguished service to the Empire. Now was it fallen upon evil days and its fortunes impoverished, hence his lowly position. He was entitled to a place in the Throne Legion, where membership was reserved to armigerous families; but it takes wealth and high position and influence to rise to anything higher than a captaincy; and these he lacked, hence his rank as a mere spearsman.

To break the uncomfortable silence, he blurted a question.

"How is it that you did not flee with the court, my lady? Did not the Queen and all her suite depart in one body?"

Lady Niane nodded wanly. She seemed distracted, staring down at the corpses. She did not at once answer, but he knew how shocking it must have been to a maiden of gentle birth—to be hunted through the echoing halls by masked and leering assassins. For he presumed any agents of Thelatha now in the palace must be spies or assassins. But this raised a small puzzle: Spies of the Dragon who had somehow infiltrated the Great

House before it was taken must have been sent upon urgent and momentous missions. Why would they turn from these simply to sate their lusts by attempting to rape a lost and helpless girl? It was rather odd. But now she spoke falteringly.

"Yes, Throne warrior, but I was in a remote sector of the Great House when the Emperor reached his decision to ab—" she swallowed "—to *abandon* the Sacred Mountain! I could not join the ladies in time."

"That is regrettable; I fear for your safety, although I shall stay with you to defend you as best I can. We must depart from the Mount as swiftly as possible. Do you know of an exit?"

She put one slim hand against her throat. Abstractly, he noticed it was a lovely, soft hand with slender fingers. And the throat, too, was slim and beautiful. He thrust such thoughts from him fiercely: this was no time to indulge in romantic thoughts.

"I . . . no," she said faintly. "I tried to rejoin the ladies, but could not make my way to them in time. Now I find myself in a sector of the palace unfamiliar to me—surely *you* must know it, warrior?"

He shook his head, blond locks tousling.

"Not I, lady! This portion of the Great House is unknown to me as well. Well, then, we shall have to search for a way out as best we can. May I carry your bundle?"

She retreated against the pillar, and her face

went pallid as the marble. It was as if he had sought to molest her person: and her reaction was curious, although he had little time to think of it now. Later, he would remember that involuntary shrinking back from his hand, and how she clutched the bundle against her breasts as if to protect it from him.

"No, I . . . it is not heavy."

"Very well," he said coldly, his tanned face stiff. Naturally, he misunderstood her withdrawal. In such conditions—the Empire breaking up, the world collapsing about them—a warrior deserting his post, a lost girl . . . some might have seized the opportunity to ravish a pretty body, like the two human beasts he had cut down. Surely, the maiden was lovely enough, slim and tall, with shallow, sweet breasts and long, supple legs, pale, sweet oval of calm face, shadowy, great eyes, long hair like a banner of black silk. She could have been no older than sixteen. And he had been long without a woman.

But he felt affronted: insulted—did she dare to dream a warrior of the Throne Legion would fall upon a helpless maiden and force his manhood upon her?

Almost, face flaming, hard anger rising within him, he turned on his heel just then to leave her to whatever fate might lie ahead. But warriors of the Throne were men of chivalry. In his despondency, he needed something to defend, to fight for. And, in any case, he would not leave a maiden of Atlantis to the squat, leering, brutal hordes of the Dragon, to paw and use.

"Come. Let us try this way."

And they went into the palace together.

vi. The Airboat

Twice Diodric and the Lady Niane narrowly escaped discovery. For there were others in the palace: rough-looking, unshaven men in rude garments of patched leather. Obviously, these were no denizens of the gigantic castle, nor more of the masked assassins, but outlaws and looters—scum from the nameless alleys of the City slums, drawn thither by the lure of fabulous plunder in the deserted palace.

The first of such they encountered were tearing up a gorgeous tapestry of glowing silks wherewith to drag a chest of silver plate. Diodric drew the girl into the shadows of a doorway so they might escape their notice. It was not, as it might seem, a cowardly action. Diodric was a gallant and courageous young swordsman, but he was not a fool: the ruffians were twelve in number, burly men, armed with stout cudgels. It would not help the Lady Niane if he were to charge valiantly into such a band and be struck down, leaving her the helpless prey to their lusts.

They eluded the looters, and followed a marble stairway that went coiling up to the third level. Here they came upon yet another palace plunderer, who took them by surprise with no chance to hide from his discovery. He had been dragging a beautiful image of the god Rhakotis from a plinth of black marble when they came blundering into the antechamber. He dropped the golden thing, made a swipe at Diodric with his cudgel, yelling obscenities. The youth ran him twice through the body, and left his corpse sprawled in a spreading crimson pool before the serene, gold face of Rhakotis, whom he restored to its pedestal. They went on, finding no looters as yet had penetrated into the upper tiers of the mammoth ziggurat.

On the third tier they discovered an astounding treasure.

Moored to a shaft of glittering feldspar, a sleek yacht of shining, silvery metal floated buoyantly under an awning of purple cloth. The shaft of crystal thrust out from the parapet of their tier, but was invisible from the tier below due to the broad lip of the tier, which was worked into a fantastic row of bird-beaked gargoyles and grotesques. Niane sucked in her breath at the very sight of the lovely, fantastic thing, and Diodric, who already began to taste the bitterness of despair and failure, took heart from this fabulous discovery.

For this graceful, weightless thing of mirror-bright metal, which bore embossed on its needle-pointed bow the insignia of a mighty House, was one of the legendary flying ships. The art of their manufacture had perished millennia ago: *viwân vidya,* as the science of the flying boats was called in the old Lemurian tongue, was one of the many casualties of time. In the dawn of man some old sorcerer of Lemuria the Lost had first learned from the High Gods the secret of the weightless metal, *urlium.* This made it possible to construct the airboats wherewith the Lemurian Kings of the Golden Empire of the Sun had spread their conquests over half of the earth in the golden days before the Mighty Motherland subsided at last into the green depths of the nameless oceans of the remote and ultimate west.

The Divine Tiongorya himself, god-king and founder of the Golden Empire, had flown in such ships what time he went up in fabulous wars against the Black City of the Magicians. And for a hundred thousand years the Emperors of the Lost Motherland had used such aerial navies to set the black-and-golden banners of High Patanga over the rose-red cities of Mayapan and the delta of Khem-Mu, the Seriadic Land to the remote east, where the Lemurians had founded their colony of Sait-ya, the City of the Great Sphinx.

But all this was legend, rumored in crumbling pages of old, forgotten books. The legend whispered, too, that it was in such aerial boats as this —*viwân,* they were called—had come the Great Migration, when Valthoth, son of Vandar, the Prince of the Last Days, had led the remnants of dying Lemuria to a new home here in the Island of Atlantis. Valthoth the Immortal had built the walls of Caiphul, first and most ancient of all the Atlantean cities, and had fathered the First Dynasty, that of the Lemurians, who had ruled all of this land until the collapse of the First Empire. "Thoth the Thrice-Great" was he known as today, and venerated as a godling by the Shemitish lords of the present dynasty who had raised the Second Empire here on the eastern shores, in the City of the Golden Gates.

But in the long ages that had rolled across this ancient land from that remote day to this, the secret of the manufacturer of the flying craft had become lost. Few, a very few, of the ancient *viwân* still survived. It was by the most incredible stroke of fortune that Diodric and the Lady Niane should have stumbled upon so rare and priceless a memento of the distant eons.

Or, perchance, it was not Blind Fortune, but the inscrutable will of the Gods.

In either case, they were saved. They—and *That* which they bore with them.

vii. The Flight from the City

"Do you know how to make it fly?" the girl asked, her luminous eyes enormous in the shadow of dusk. The boy shrugged, with a laugh.

"Since we must fly the *viwân* or perish here," he said coldly, "we will fly!"

They approached the slim, graceful aerial yacht. The rear deck was surrounded by a low rail, and this Diodric caught, springing up lithely and drawing himself aboard. The floating deck trembled and swung under his weight, but the craft remained buoyant. Coiled in a trap door under the rear deck, he found a rope ladder which one could attach to the deck rail by clamps. He snapped it into place and tossed it over the side so that the girl could clamber up. The long skirts of her blue gown tangled about her legs and made climbing difficult; the cumbersome bundle of garments and personal possessions to which she clung made it difficult for her to use her hands. But she curtly refused his suggestion to pass the bundle up to him first. Instead, she struggled up the ladder while Diodric, sourly watching, cursed her for a simple-minded fool: did she think *he* wanted to rummage through her few pitiful belongings? It was incomprehensible, but she still did not trust him. With all the treasures of the palace about them—why would he want to paw through her miserable dresses and jewelry?

Helping her over the rail, Diodric led the girl forward into the snug little cabin. Two wall bunks were set therein, one to either side of the small cabin. Forward, under the curved pane of glass windows, lay the control console, with a great chair that was fastened to the floor. The girl sat

trembling on one of the twin bunks, and Diodric
went forward to seat himself before the controls.
He studied them, frowning thoughtfully. There
would not be much time. If a gang of looters were
to ascend to this level, and surprise them, all would
be lost. And, from far below, he could faintly hear
the thunder of assault as the warriors of the Green
Dragon swept the first parapet at last with all their
irresistible thousands.

In theory, Diodric knew the method of control.
The airboats had long, slim, streamlined hulls.
Great engines were concealed below deck, running the length of the hull. Protruding below the
pointed nose before him, and the tapering tail behind him, were powerful rotors whose whirling
blades somehow thrust against the impalpable
texture of the air itself, and by which the vessel
could be driven. Somewhere in the depths of the
engines, a bank of curious crystals gave power to
turn these blades. *Sithurls*—"sun-stones"—the Lemurians of old had called them; for in some mysterious and magical fashion, these power crystals
drew energy from sunlight itself, stored it, focused
it, and used it to drive the engines.

Brow knotted in puzzlement, the young warrior bent over the console, fingering the controls
hesitantly. Strange glyphs were painted in scarlet
enamel on the light, wooden panel of the console;
but Diodric could not read the Lemurian characters. The controls were few and simple enough: a
row of throttles which were metal levers in sunken
slots; the glass sphere of the directional gauge,

wherein a pendulum of lodestone swung ever to the north; and a round wheel which (he guessed) must control the adjustable vanes of the tail and somehow swing the craft in different directions by pushing against the airstream.

But the question that went through his mind was: how do you make the engines start in the first place?

He had best discover the secret—and swiftly!

For as he bent, frowning over the controls—twenty unshaven looters burst onto the parapet and swept, howling with glee, upon them!

Shock went ripping through Diodric like a thrown spear! Involuntarily, he thrust out his hand and thrust home a central lever. A thrumming vibration sprang to life in the decks beneath him. The *viwân* quivered now like a live thing under his hand. Tentatively, he reached out for the great wheel.

A roar awoke among the massed looters pelting toward them. Thrown cudgels thumped and slammed the glistening metallic hull of the airboat. The foremost of the ragged crew, a burly and vicious-faced lout with a snarling mouth and hot, angry eyes, leapt up from the marble floor, seizing the deck rail with one hand. In his other hand, a naked scimitar caught the last embers of sunset in a liquid flash of ruby fire.

And in that same instant the whirling rotor blades engaged and the glittering craft floated away from the tier. For only a moment it tugged at the end of its anchor rope, still securely tied about the feldspar rod. Then the line snapped with an audible twang and the boat shot into thin air, drifting aimlessly high above the sacred City. It swerved and eddied under the fumbling guidance of Diodric's inexperienced hand—then shot away to the west in a shallow, wobbling glide.

With an unearthly screech of blood-chilling horror, the dangling ruffian felt his fingers loosen as the rising wind slid along the curves of the hull and plucked him away. He flew off behind the hurtling craft like a huge, ungainly leaf torn loose by raging winds. In an instant, he was lost in the mists and roiling smoke that hung low over the City.

viii. The City of the Golden Gates

By now they were far above the City—perhaps half a mile aloft. Sweating, hands trembling with tension, the young Throne warrior clung to the controls. There is an uncanny terror to flight—a sense of horror at leaving the solid earth behind and venturing into giddy heights of empty air. But, and swiftly, this fear dwindled as Diodric discovered that he could manipulate the controls. He experimented, learning how to send the ship curving off to either side—how to send it leaping ahead under a spurt of power—and how to slacken its forward velocity by throwing the drag of the prow rotors into force.

He looked down through the curving crystal pane at the splendid panorama of the City below. His eyes searched the gloom, reading familiar landmarks. In that mighty and fabulous metropolis, founded in the most remote antiquity, he and his race had dwelt from the beginning of their House. Therein had he been born—the spires of his ancestral palace could be clearly seen even from this height. He looked long upon the City of the Golden Gates. He knew that it might be years before he saw it again, the golden capital of his childhood. He knew, as well, that never in this life might he again stride its streets or see the glorious acropolis of the sacred Mount.

There were ten cities in Atlantis—but only one City.

It was built on the east coast of the continent, close to the shores of the Gorgonian Sea. The metropolis was built in a perfect circle some fifteen miles in diameter. In the center of the City rose the sacred Mount. Upon this height, in the beginning, the God Pazadon the Lord of the Sea had fathered the Divine Dynasty of the Atlantides on the body of the maid Cleito. This sacred spot was now enshrined within the great Temple dedicated to the Sea Lord and the Mother of Kings. The walls thereof were sheathed in silver and the ten pinnacles in fiery gold. Leading down from the Temple of Pazadon to the base of the Mount, which was not overly high, stretched the Sacred

Stair of a Thousand Steps. Behind the Temple, the Grove of Pazadon stood, the ancient trees somber in the dying light. To one side of the Temple rose the Great House, the mightiest structure ever raised by the hands of men, like a tremendous tiered pyramid. Lesser temples, palaces, and administrative structures clustered about the sides of the Mount, and around its base was a wall sheathed in orichalcum, the holy metal that sparkled like red fire.

The three waterways that formed concentric rings around the base of the acropolis hill glimmered faintly in the gloom. The outermost of these circular moats was broad and deep, and even from this height, Diodric could see the tall masts of the great triremes moored at stone docks therein.

On the circular zone of land between the middle and the outermost of the waterways rose the great Hippodrome, the famous racecourse, where chariot teams sought the coveted victory chaplet. He could also observe the Baths of Eumelos beyond. The zones of land that alternated with the waterways bore lesser palaces, the mansions of the nobility, the barracks of the Throne Legion, groves and gardens. Each zone of land was walled, rendering the Mount a triple-walled citadel. Beyond the Wall of Orichalc the next zone was walled with a shining metal called *kassiteros;* the outermost wall was sheathed with plates of brass.

Outside the great waterways in which laboring generations of Atlanteans had confined the river on whose estuary the City of the Golden Gates had first arisen, the suburbs fell away to the City wall itself, a towering rampart of snowy marble. Here innumerable houses were ranked. These were built of black, red, or white stone, a dazzling pattern of colors.

From this height, the damage of war somewhat concealed by the glamor of nightfall, the City of the Golden Gates was an awesome spectacle of incredible splendor. No city had ever been so great in all the eons of time: not Patanga the Great in olden, lost Lemuria; not Tarshish of the Silver Throne in faraway splendor on the coasts of the Thurian continent to the east.

Beautiful, beautiful beyond thought, the king-city of Atlantis lay in the gloaming.

Already the streams of green-clad, swarthy Dragon warriors thronged the streets. Flames flickered in many windows. Plumes of oily black smoke dirtied the clear twilight. Through the great fallen gates the conquering legions poured. Diodric could faintly hear the drone of the ray projectors and the rumble of collapsing walls as Dragon warriors, armed with the Black Fire, buried small pockets of resistance under sliding tons of rubble. Already most of the larger buildings of the outer City lay either in heaps of smoking ruin or stood wrapped in weird dark flames. A distant many-throated roar of triumph rose to him where he hovered, and he knew the Conqueror had entered into the City, and Imperial Atlantis was fallen in this hour.

He touched the controls and the airboat

scudded before the wind. He circled the City of the Golden Gates once, in a last farewell; then he flew away into the west and was lost to the sight of men below as darkness covered the earth with black wings.

And thus the Long Night came down on the glory of High Atlantis in its golden prime. The Long Night which the dying warrior had prophesied. The Long Night that hath no ending.

ix. The Green-Robed One

Darkness and silence filled the deserted ziggurat that was the Great House. And dark night reigned beyond the towering, nine-tiered mountain of the palace. The night was thick and smothering, and the clear face of the Lady of Heaven was hidden, this night, from men. Even the stars burned faint and few.

Over the dead, deserted City in blackest night, one terrible star burned with evil crimson fire. And sorcerers, bent over crumbling Lemurian scrolls of pterodactyl-skin parchment, whispered the name *Azphar*, Star of Evil.

The marble parapets were bare save for corpses.

The streets were littered with the dead, and strewn with wreckage.

Houses, temples, palaces, burned or lay vacant in the darkness.

But there was one who lived and he went prowling through the echoing vastness of the Great House. Robed all in emerald green he went, and there were gloves of green silk on his hands, and a cowled cloak of green was drawn about his gaunt, hunched shoulders, and the hood thereof was closely drawn about his face so that no eye might perceive his visage and know his likeness, no more than any man living knew his Name or his dark and terrible Lineage.

Like a green shadow, this man prowled through the great halls and crept down the vast stairways of marble and glided through the chambers, suites, apartments, and hallways of the deserted palace.

Hovering above his left shoulder a Witchlight spread about him a glowing sphere of illumination. At times this floating globe of cold gray leprous fire cast the shadow of the robed and hooded one before him, black, batlike, and monstrous upon the walls.

Slowly the burning red eye of Azphar ascended the enshadowed vault. As it ascended, the green-robed one seemed to become taller and mightier, until at length he strode the marble ways with the grinding iron weight of a great conqueror and stood tall and unbent like a mighty king. It was as if he drew vigor and sustenance from the ascendancy of the Star of Evil.

Behind the shadows of the hood, a veil of thinnest green silk overlay his features. Not even his *eyes* could be seen through the gauze covering. But they were cold and merciless and cruel and cunning, those hidden eyes. They searched every corner of every room, and nothing there was that could escape their grim scrutiny.

In his gloved left hand, the stalker amid the shadows bore a great staff of dark green wood. And the tree wherefrom that wood cometh is no tree of this earth, aye, and of the dreadful *fruit* of that tree let no child of man inquire.

At length the black, batlike shadow of the Silent Walker glided ghostlike across a mighty portal of sacred orichalcum that burned like red silver in the cold gray fires of the Witchlight. At this portal, the Stalker paused. No sound came from the veiled and hidden face, but the unearthly scrutiny of those hidden eyes swooped to fasten at once upon the strange sigil set upon the double leaves of that shining portal.

This sigil was in the form of a Nonagram—the Star of Nine Rays. A holy and terrific emblem, this Nine-Pointed Sign. It was set with fierce rubies and polished but uncut diamonds within the shining metal.

Like a tendril of mist, the gloved right hand was thrust out, pointing at the door.

And, although no Word audible to human ears was spoken, the still atmosphere of the great Hall of a Hundred Columns quaked as if disturbed by Syllables of Power.

Groaning, as if in protest, the valves of that great portal swung inward. And the green-robed one hovered for a moment upon the threshold . . . then glided within.

Austere were the furnishings of that mighty room, but they were of the richest substances. Opals and globules of pure amber studded a great crystal plinth. The air was holy with nard and myrrh and rarest frankincense.

The shadow glided toward the crystal plinth, which was veiled beneath a shadowy canopy of thick, soft velvet.

Glided forward—only to halt.

For the smooth upper surface of the glistening plinth was—*empty*.

For a long, breathless moment the green shadow hovered, glaring with burning eyes of unseen fire at the vacant surface. Then, with a swift and terrible motion, the green-gloved hand brandished the staff of emerald wood and there sounded a deafening retort as the crystal exploded into ten thousand ringing shards.

Then it was that the green shadow spoke.

Only one word did the robed one speak. But the sound of that voice, grating and harsh and metallic, could never have been uttered by a completely human throat.

There was a throttled rage, and a heart-deep anguish, and a ferocious and terrible lust in that croaking, ghastly voice.

"Gone!" it said, and: "*Gone!*" And: "*GONE!*"

Then the Witchlight flared up suddenly—blindingly—and winked out, plunging the room into sudden and absolute darkness.

And the room, like the ruined plinth, was— empty.

✶ 2 ✶

The Book of Niane

In this manner were the warlike affairs
of the Royal City disposed. But those
of the other nine cities in a different
manner. Each of the Ten Kings possessed absolute authority over the men
and the laws in his own city. But the
government of these kings were con-
formable to the laws given by Poseidon,
of which the greatest was this: That
they should never wage war against
each other, but should make war
should any person endeavor to extir-
pate the Royal Race . . . for they as-
signed the Empire to the dynasty of
the Atlantides.

—PLATO: The *Timaeus*, 119.C, 120.B

i. Niane's Dream

Worn out by the trials and exertions of the day, the Lady Niane slept huddled on one of the small bunks along the walls of the airboat's cabin, while Diodric, seated before the controls, kept the craft arrowing into the night.

As she slept, her hands did not loosen: they were tightly clenched about the bundle of belongings which she hugged to her young breasts. And in this sleep, which was at first fitful and troubled, but which gradually deepened until she lay in the very depths of exhausted slumber, there came to her a dream.

It seemed to Niane that her mind sped back through time to a point earlier in the day. She saw herself in the vast emptiness of the almost deserted palace. She watched as the Niane of her dream— whom she observed as if it were another person

—busily, with shaking hands, gathered together a few garments and belongings, and hurried from her chambers to join the Queen and her ladies.

It was strange, this dream: ghostly and enchanted. She could see all with vague clarity, although the details of the vision were blurred and distorted, as if seen through a warped glass window. But no sound at all could she hear: everything transpired in an utter and frightening silence, like the illusions conjured up by an enchanter.

The corridors of the lower palace were thronged by fleeing nobles and courtiers. Through the madly streaming crowd, the Lady Niane wandered lost and affrighted. Time and again she sought to stay one of the fleeing courtiers or men-at-arms, to ask from which landing stage the Emperor and his party were departing. For it was the rumor that the Divine Pnomphis would flee the City, not by land, but by the few remaining flying craft his dynasty treasured and preserved as a rare heritage of Lost Lemuria, from whose godlike race the Dynasty, according to tradition, was sprung.

But none of the fleeing throng would pause and answer her; distracted by fear, dreading that any moment the hordes of the Demon King would invest the Great House, they sped in all directions, seeking little-used postern gates and other exits. Some were bound for the long quays of marble, where gilded gondolas gave chance of flight by means of the system of canals. Others were bound for a land passage through the great

Necropolis beyond the City to the south. And each person she stopped shrugged off her hand. Some, in greater panic, thrust her aside rudely and with threatening words.

So at length it came to pass that the Lady Niane wandered lost and alone through the deserted palace, and found herself in the mighty Hall of a Hundred Columns. All about, through the gloom, colossal stone pillars, whose rondures were graven with the names, cartouches, dignities, and exploits of the mighty kings of the race of the Atlantides, soared aloft to support an arched ceiling far above.

Upon many past occasions had Niane visited this spacious hall which was but an antechamber to the colossal Court of the Pylons wherein it was the wont of the sacred Emperors to hold sway upon the Throne of Atlantis. But always before, this hall had been thronged with a glittering and superb assemblage of the nobility and the priesthood and the court. Now it lay empty: vast, echoing, and sunken in shadows.

Dwarfed by the towering height of the pillars, the girl wandered from column to column, weeping and frightened.

Then, from afar, she espied a sprawled figure whose gorgeous raiment was all one welter of streaming gore. He lay before the mighty portals of a doorway whose leaves were plated with the sacred orichalcum which flashed with red light. And upon the portals of this door was a symbol set in twinkling gems, a Nine-Rayed Star. By this potent and terrific emblem she knew this to be the Chamber of the Hallows, a most sacred place.

She ventured nearer, moved by pity of the dying man, and saw that she knew him by his silver mane and majestic beard. He was old, but he had the might and stature of a mighty warrior. She, in her lowly station, had never conversed with him before, since he was one of the highest of the lords. Rhamsheth Asterion was his name, the Lord Guardian of the Holies. Coming nearer, she perceived that he had taken a great wound in the belly. His large hands were clamped on this wound, as if to hold back by the strength of his hand the life that bled slowly, in streams of hot crimson, between his clenched fingers. But she saw also that some life yet lingered within his mighty frame. A red trail passed under the close leaves of the door, and she saw the red imprint of his wet hands upon the leaves, where he had closed them behind him. Sprawled in a pool of gore some yards away, lay the body of another man in black whose face was masked.

She knelt to ask if she could assist him. He peered up blearily at her, then, of a sudden, his eyes cleared. They searched her face with the fierce unblinking gaze of a great hawk, and one of the wet, red hands came up to clasp her wrist in an iron grip.

Then, in the dream, it seemed that she could hear the converse that had passed between the two of them, but faint and far off:

"Bend closer, girl, let me see your face . . . ah,

you are one of the Royal ladies: I have seen you betimes in the company of the Queen," he said, and his speech came forth in great gasps, as if he dragged the words up out of a well of silence with prodigious effort.

He brushed her offers of aid aside bruskly, still clutching her by the wrist.

"No time for words now, girl. I am sped, but ere I go down to the Kingdom of Darkness I must pass a terrible burden into your hands: alas, that it be so, but thus it must be, for I am near the end of my strength and there is none other here to take up That which I can no longer shield," he panted, and she wondered at his strange, portentous words.

ii. It Passeth to Niane

His fierce eyes searched her pale, tear-stained face with a desperate urgency. He gasped for breath; and all the while his life leaked from the terrible wound in his belly.

"Girl, what is thy name . . . Niane, of the House of Phiodon . . . aye, I knew your late father, girl . . . loyal unto death was he to his Emperor . . . art thou any the less loyal? Speak, lass, and true, as you fear the Gods!"

Falteringly, she told him she was true and loyal to the Divine Dynasty. At this, his urgency subsided a little, and he mumbled under his breath, and sagged in her arms a little, as if his strength ebbed. But once again the fierce flame blazed up in his clouded eyes, and the brave old warrior lord fought death off from him for a few more moments.

"Listen to me, girl. Even now I came unto the Chamber to remove therefrom the Hallows it doth hold, and found another—" his head jerked contemptuously at the unknown figure sprawled some yards distant "—reaching for That which no hand may touch, save the hand appointed . . . him I struck down in the sacred place, but from his venomed sword I took a wound which even now steals my strength away . . . ere I die I pass This to you, for there is none other to whom I may give this Thing . . ."

His eyes blazed in his worn and ravaged face, which was pale as marble to the lips; and the strength of his hand on her wrist was a crushing strength.

Taking his hand away, he plucked Something from the bosom of his robes and thrust it under her eyes. At the sight of the Thing which he held she voiced a small cry and would have recoiled in holy awe, save that his other hand grasped her wrist again, and dragged her near.

"Girl! You know the meaning of this Thing? I read it within thine eyes . . . then take It, child, I pass It unto you . . . even I, Rhamsheth Asterion, who am Lord and Guardian thereof . . . listen,

girl: the White Emperor will take flight into the
cities of the west . . . but he will meet with be-
trayal, for treachery is all about, aye, the Empire
fell through treachery . . . the Naked Sword of War
went forth from the Great House to the Ten Kings
of Atlantis, and lo! but three of the cities lent
their host to the defense of the Throne, as *all* are
bidden by the Pillar of the Law . . . as *all* are sworn
before the altars of Lord Pazadon to do in time of
need . . . treachery . . . black treachery!"

With a last surge of his ebbing strength, the
Lord Guardian thrust the Hallow into her shrinking fingers and fell back gasping.

"Pnomphis is doomed . . . death hovers on black
wings to take his spirit . . . but the Queen is with
child . . . I pray the Gods it be a boy, to take up
the fallen Standard and rally the loyal Atlanteans
. . . and hearken, girl! Into no hands must you give
up That which I have passed to you . . . only to the
Emperor or to his Queen, or to a loyal son of the
Divine Dynasty . . . thy life must be spent to defend That which now you hold . . . *and at every
cost, It must be kept from the clutches of the
Dragon!*"

The crimson gushed from his white lips and his
eyes went blank as stone, and the Last Guardian
fell dead on the threshold of the Chamber of the
Hallows.

And trembling with fear, her slim body torn
with a tempest of weeping, the girl stowed away
with shaking fingers into the midst of her bundled

garments the Thing which had been passed to her by the hand of the dying man.

A frightful and momentous responsibility was now hers: her slender shoulders must bear a terrible burden; but there was none other worthy to bear that burden.

Then, as the dream of Niane faded, she watched as the two terrible men, clothed in black and masked as had been the spy Lord Rhamsheth had caught in the Chamber and had slain, came upon her and raised a howling cry, and she watched herself flee in terror through the wilderness of echoing stone until they sprang upon her at the tier. And there it was the young Throne warrior had found her and saved her from the agents of the Dragon who would tear from her the Thing she bore . . .

iii. The Mountains

Azphar soared high in the black zenith of night. At length it passed from its height and faded from the vision of men.

The Lady of Heaven, the great golden Moon of Atlantis, thrust aside her veil of vapors and spread her gentle light over the stricken and desolate land.

Niane awoke suddenly. A hand had shaken her shoulder. She clutched for the precious bundle but it was still there. It was only her young defender who had aroused her, saying the night was near done and a great weariness was upon him from the exertions of the day's battle, and that he could no longer thrust sleep from him, but must rest.

She nodded, and rose to her feet.

"Where are we now?" she asked faintly.

He shrugged. "Only the Gods know; the night is thick and I can see no landmark familiar to me. But we are in the mountains, wherefor I dare not remain longer aloft, lest I fall asleep at the controls and our craft strike the peaks. It is my thought to moor the *viwân* here on the heights, that we both may slumber without danger of collision. What think you on this, lady?"

Falteringly, Niane said something to the effect that his decision seemed to be sound. The moon was rising now, shedding pale rays by which terrible walls of jagged black stone were illuminated if but dimly. The harsh and broken cliffs were all about them, but the ancient Lemurian craft could ascend to no greater height than this. The girl shuddered as she gazed down the giddy chasms that fell away beneath them to fearful depths; she felt contemptuous of her own fearful timidity, and wished she could draw upon some source of courage to sustain her. But the terrors of the day, the dreadful calamity that had brought the very

Empire down in ruin, her abandonment by all
those she knew and loved, and the grim and awful
responsibility which had inexorably devolved upon
her—all these things conspired to exhaust what
little courage dwelt in her girlish heart.

She stole a glance sidewise between silken
lashes at the young warrior whom fate had thrust
into proximity with her, and whom necessity had
made her companion. Diodric: it was a good name,
a Celtic name and of another people than the
Divine Dynasty, which was Shemitish in origin;
she, herself, was of Turanian blood, but she had
dwelt so long amongst the Shemite lords of the
present Dynasty that she had come to share their
dislike of foreign blood.

He had a good face, she thought: young, perhaps the same age as herself, or but a trifle older;
very serious of expression, and drawn and pale now
with fatigue; but there was strength and strong
will in the stubborn line of the jaw, and breeding
and intelligence in the broad brow and clear eyes.

She was aware of a stiffness in his manner toward her, and equally conscious of a constraint in
her manner toward him. It was not that she did
not trust him: it was that she scarcely dared trust
any person, so valuable and important was That
which she bore. She must have offended him by
shrinking from his touch, by holding aloof from
his assistance, by snatching the precious bundle
away from his helpful hands. But, in all conscience, she had intended no offense: again she
cursed her girlish weakness.

"There!" he cried suddenly, pointing.

The pallid shafts of the moon had illuminated a level surface of glassy rock: a sterile scarp whereon a broken spire of crystal thrust up from the mass of glittering black gneiss. It was for such a protuberance he had been searching: a place where he could in safety moor the *viwân*.

Now, with patient, careful hands, he lightly guided the hovering craft into the proximity of the spar. Springing lightly from the cabin to the rear deck, he fashioned with agile fingers a running noose from the broken length of line which was fastened to a mooring ring locked to the tail assembly. After several tries, he managed to secure the noose about the spear of shining crystalline rock.

The girl watched him with covert eyes from the door of the cabin. He had put aside his cumbersome breastplate whereon the Sun emblem of the Throne Legion was emblazoned with goldwork. His greaves and girdle had likewise been discarded for comfort, and he went clothed only in a short tunic of supple black leather which ended at mid-thigh. Niane looked upon his strong, muscular arms and bare brown legs in their thonged sandals, his deep chest and broad shoulders. He was handsome, strong, and young, she thought, and far more attractive than the effete and subtle courtiers she had known: they were languid, drawling, perfumed fops; this was a *man*.

They would fly on into the west, with morning. But for the hours of night that remained, they would rest and sleep, and prepare themselves for whatever hardships and perils the future held.

It was fortunate for the unruffled serenity of their slumbers that they could not know the full extent of those perils.

iv. In the Clutch of the Troglodytes

Night ended at last, and dawn stained the eastern sky with a rosy flush of faint light which grew gradually stronger. Shafts of golden radiance thrust like bronze spears into the dark heavens, driving Night from his domain.

Cold dank mist arose from the fields and meadows. Dew flashed like tiny diamonds on the greensward and upon the leaves of the great trees in the dark forests of Atlantis. Day was come. An Empire and an Age had fallen yesterday in flame and thunder; now a new day was here, and it dawned upon a changed and mysterious world filled with strange new things, where Evil ruled and the Dragon of the Abyss held sway.

Niane awoke all at once, like a startled forest creature, to the ringing sound of a great cry.

She started up and gazed with horror at the evil, leering faces that peered in through the crystal panes. Diodric stood at the door of the cabin, hurling the strength of his shoulders against it. It was his cry of shock and alarm which had aroused her from her sleeping.

She looked again and saw with a thrill of pure horror that crawling things had crept forth from the clefts and fissures of the mountain during the reign of darkness. Weird, stunted little beings had stealthily bound the airship about with many turnings of tough leather strips, and now the *viwân* was pinned and helpless against the glassy scarp. And the dwarfed and swart little creatures that went capering like immense obscene toads across the decks and over the nose of their craft, were hammering with filthy hands against the windows, seeking entry.

"What *are* those—things?" she cried.

Diodric turned a grim, set face toward her.

"Troglodytes—curse the luck!" the youth growled. "I had not known they infested these mountains—we must have flown further in the night than ever I had thought—these must be the Mountains of the Terror."

The Mountains of the Terror! Her flesh crept at the thought. She had, betimes, heard horrid tales whispered of these vile and murderous dwarfs and of the loathsome practices wherewith they loved to wreak their vengeance upon the Big People, as they called ordinary human beings.

Some said the Troglodytes were monstrous and deformed men sprung from human loins, but degraded into bestiality through some curse of the Gods. Others hinted that the malignant and stunted little monsters were the original inhabitants of Atlantis, who had been driven under-ground by the coming of mankind to this isle.

Whatever their source and origin, the hideous and repulsive little creatures populated a distant mountain range in ever-increasing numbers. Buried in the black bowels of the mountains, they swarmed and bred like vermin. And horrible beyond measure were the fates of the unwary and foolish travelers who ventured into those forbidding peaks. A full cohort of Atlantean warriors had once ventured into the Mountains of the Terror, sworn to stamp out the swarming Dwellers in the Depths. The mountains had swallowed up all the tall glittering warriors and they were never seen again.

"What are you going to do?" the girl whispered.

His face was pale and twisted and there was desperation in his eyes.

"I must go out and cut the thongs with my sword. We cannot lift the craft against the bindings they have wrapped about it."

"But—how will you avoid the—the things waiting out there?" she faltered.

To this question he had no ready answer. He must fight them off as best he could, and pray the luck of the Gods went with him.

"There must be something *I* can do," the girl gasped. But he only compressed his lips and shook his head.

"We have only one sword. You have nothing with which to defend yourself, save that dagger at your waist. And it is best that you remain here within."

There was no arguing with Diodric, and the girl felt a strange helplessness as she watched him prepare for the ordeal. He tore his cloak into broad strips and wound these about his face, arms and legs, donning the cuirass that would shield his chest and his back. The wicked, leering, capering little monstrosities were armed with knives of bone and sharp bits of rock and cudgels of heavy wood: the cloth wrappings would, at least, afford him some slight protection from the assault of these.

He thrust the cabin door open, bursting the thongs that bound it shut, and sprang out upon the rear deck. Dawnlight flashed on the shining sword as if caught by a polished mirror. The sword flickered once, twice, clearing the deck to his left and his right.

And the battle was joined.

v. The Deep

The snarling little men were squat and deformed, with bowed, waddling legs and long apelike arms. Although they were small, they were fearsomely strong, for great bulging knots of muscle swelled in arm and chest and shoulder. Their heads were flattish, matted with filthy hair. They had gray, leathern skin, dank and unwholesome and crusted with mire. They went naked as beasts, and the small squinting red eyes that peered from their misshapen and repulsive features were murky with the bloodlust of the beast.

They swept in a chittering horde upon him. Diodric took a deep breath, planted his feet squarely, and swung his sword in a great sweeping arc. The razor-keen steel sheared through hands and limbs, and hurled them back, mewling and spitting with mingled rage, frustration, and pain.

In the interval, he set his sword against the thongs that were woven about the rear deck and snapped them. Ten or a dozen he severed in this manner, with swift strokes, ere the chittering horde swept down upon him again.

This time the arc of his glittering sword left a gory tracery hanging momentarily on the dawn-bright air: a dribble of scarlet droplets followed the line of its course as it shore through the repulsive little monsters.

But they were upon him. Horny hands clamped around foot, leg, and hip. One filthy arm encircled his throat from behind. Another clung, chattering and grimacing like some malignant cat, its arms and legs wrapped around his sword arm.

He went down under a heaving, wriggling mound of the Troglodytes. Fetid breath blew stinking in his face from snarling, drooling lips that writhed back in a fighting grimace to reveal the yellow stumps of rotting fangs. Red eyes glared in bestial menace at him through tangled and filthy locks.

As Niane watched, hands clutching the hilt of her dagger, face pale with terror, the wriggling heap of filthy, twisted bodies convulsed—and exploded apart. Diodric staggered into view, hammering about him with the sword. The swathings had been torn from his limbs and they glistened wetly with blood from many small wounds and scratches. His face was streaming with blood also, from an ugly cut in his scalp, but other than this he seemed unharmed. His steel cuirass was nicked and scratched and dented.

Kicking with sandaled feet, smashing Troglodytes aside with knees and elbows, the grim-faced young warrior battled his way forward, where he swept his sword—which now was one welter of trickling crimson from cross hilt to blade tip—in great sweeping scythelike circles, clearing space around him. And again the flashing blade slashed through leathern thongs. Huddled shaking in the cabin, Niane could feel the craft quiver and bob up slightly from the peak as the bonds which held it parted one by one.

But then she tensed as a spasm of fear ripped through her. She saw, although Diodric did not, the wicked gleaming eyes of a hulking Troglodyte as it clambered up the prow of the *viwân*. Clutched in one gnarled fist was a cudgel of heavy knotted wood. Thews stretched and tightened. The apelike arm swung back, and flung the cudgel straight at the back of Diodric's skull.

The club crashed against his head and it seemed to Diodric that his brain exploded in a shower of white-hot sparks. Dimly he was aware of the deck swinging up toward his face, but then all thought expired and he fell forward into the depths of darkness as if thrust down into the Deep.

With her heart sinking under a smother of terrors, the Lady Niane watched as the repulsive, twittering horde slithered and scrambled in a crawling wave over the body of Diodric and he vanished from her view.

Then, in the next instant, dwarfed bodies thudded against the cabin door. It crashed open, and filthy loping things poured within the cabin. She swung out, gashing the face of one leering dwarf with her dagger and it fell backwards, squalling in pain. But hands were all over her now, ripping at her garments, tearing the precious bundle from her clutch and tossing it across the room.

She was conscious of the clutch of many hands, dragging her down into darkness. As she fell fainting in the hands of the grinning Troglodytes, her only thought was of the bundle which had been torn at last from her fingers and of the precious and holy Thing that now was taken from her.

And then she knew nothing at all, save the blackness about her.

vi. In the Pits

He was conscious of movement, of the pressure of bonds, and of rough walls of stone that rasped against the raw flesh of his arms and thighs as he was dragged past them.

That, and darkness, and cold, and of a vast and aching pain that throbbed in his skull like the beating of a red heart of flame: and every pulse thereof sent a red wave of agony throbbing through his body.

Diodric awoke blearily, and saw that he was a captive in the clutches of the Troglodytes.

They had wound about him many thongs of raw leather, whereby his legs were pinned together and his arms were bound helpless to his sides. The Troglodytes half-carried, half-dragged him along, and so small were the repulsive little monsters, that it took three of them to bear him.

A dim light beat down through murky shadows.

By the faint illuminance, whose source Diodric could not ascertain, he perceived that he was being borne down a narrow path that spiraled into the depths of the earth. To his left was only empty air: a colossal circular shaft, like the interior of some gigantic volcano, around whose inner wall this narrow and sloping ledge coiled downwards into the depths.

A faint whimpering cry came to his ears. Twisting his neck about, Diodric saw with a sinking heart that the Lady Niane was also captive, and was being half-dragged along in the clutches of grunting Troglodytes. He spat a curse from dry lips crusted with dust: he had hoped the girl would have had sense enough to quench the bright glitter of her dagger blade in her breast when she saw him taken, rather than to permit herself to fall alive into the hands of these loutish and depraved little monstrosities. For he had a terrible inkling of the unutterable uses to which the grimy and chittering little horde would put the body of a beautiful young woman. His stomach churned at the sickening thought.

For the space of some two or three hours the two captives were borne down into the depths of the earth by the Troglodytes. The dim light and the unchangeful vista and the grim monotony of the descent were stupefying to the senses: Diodric, ever after, had the feeling he had dozed or swooned for long periods of the interminable time.

But at length they left the ledge, which continued to uncoil slowly downward to unguessable depths, and debouched into a side cavern which opened from the wall of the immense shaft. Here the dwarfish little throng could move at a swifter pace, their horned, splayed feet pattering along through the scum of cold slime wherewith the black tunnel was carpeted.

Through a branching maze of black or dimly lit caverns the two helpless captives were dragged. Some were black as death and cold as night; others were flushed with a fiery glow, and the air of these stank sulphurously, as though volcanic fires were just beyond the searing-hot stone walls; still others were thronged with uncanny forests of pallid and unwholesome fungi, which shed a leprous cold light over the rocky walls.

Diodric felt his hopes wane with every new tunnel they entered. Even were they so fortunate as somehow to break free of their loathsome little captors, he knew with a dreadful inner certainty that he could never retrace his way through this nightmarish labyrinth to the surface again.

He feared that only Death could liberate them from the subterranean dominions of the Troglodytes.

Although the depth whereto they had now descended was awful and prodigious, and the cold wet chill and darkness would seem inimical to life, Diodric perceived that these cavernous ways were not devoid of life.

The mouths of certain side tunnels into which they did not enter were, he observed, blocked by vast webs. The strands thereof were often of the thickness of the little finger on his hand, and Diodric felt his scalp prickle and his nape hairs rise as he attempted to imagine the terrible and swollen size of the spider that could have spun so titanic a web.

In the mouths of certain other tunnels, mere wells of yawning blackness, he saw tiny, malignant red eyes observing their passage; and there came to his ears the clitter and scraping of tiny claws against rough stone.

And once they passed over a narrow stone bridge that arched above a sickening gulf. Peering over, Diodric felt his heart freeze as he stared down into the dim depths at *the colossal Worm* that lay coiled, vast and slumberous, in the Pit beneath.

After some hours, they came to a row of open chambers whose mouths were barred with thick iron. The naked horde paused before this row of cells, and a door squeaked open on rust-eaten hinges.

Into this black opening a dozen hands thrust the forms of Diodric and the Lady Niane, still bound and helpless. Then the massy gate clanged shut, was locked with a great key, and the chittering mob went pattering away into the dark silences.

vii. Captives of the Troglodytes

It took Diodric the better part of an hour to fumble clear of the leathern thongs wherewith the dwarfed little monstrosities had bound him. The rawhide thongs were tough and elastic, but the Troglodytes had tied them poorly. And, even with his hands and fingers numb from the loss of circulation, Diodric found it not difficult to untie the loose, clumsy knots and set himself free.

Once he was loose of the bonds, he hastened to untie the girl. She was in a sorry state: most of her clothing had been torn from her, although she did not seem to have suffered any injury save the insulting touch of cold, sly hands. But she was bruised and sore and bone-weary, and the terror of their desperate and lonely captivity had driven her into a state bordering on hysteria. After he had set her free, and chafed her limbs to help restore circulation, he soothed and comforted her as best he might, with awkward words and hopeful phrases, and the simple comfort of his physical nearness.

She sobbed as if her heart were emptying itself —a heart heavily charged with tears—while he embraced and petted her and soothed and gentled her with quiet words and reassurances. At length she had cried her fears away, and fell into an exhausted sleep in his arms.

For a long time he did not dare to move lest he awaken her, although his limbs were stiff and sore from holding the same position. At last he discerned that her slumbers were deep, and he gently disengaged her arms from his neck, and settled her as best he might. He tried to turn his eyes away from the bare beauty of her slender white body, which was copiously revealed through the rents in her raiment.

Then he prowled the stone hole into which they had been thrown.

He tested every inch of the barred gate. The iron rods were old and scaly with red rust, but they were two inches thick and deeply imbedded in the stone sockets cut in the floor. The door was a grille set in a heavy iron rim. The lock was unreachable. It would take the strength of ten men such as the young warrior to have dislodged a single bar of that massive gate, and at length he despaired and turned from it to search the cavern.

The stone cell was not natural, he soon saw. It had been rudely chiseled out of solid stone with infinite labor. It was no more than ten feet high and the width and depth were about the same distance.

Not even a worm could have crawled through any of the tiny cracks, interstices, or fissures his searching fingers found.

They were imprisoned beyond all hope of escape. He sat back with bowed shoulders slumped

against the wet rock as the utter hopelessness of
their situation gradually sank into his consciousness. Only a miracle of the Gods could free them
from this accursed hole.

And, after a time, there being nothing else to
do, he slept. But it was a fitful and uneasy sleep,
filled with nightmares.

viii. The Words of Ningg

At long intervals, the sound of pattering feet would
sound in the passage beyond their cell, and a dark
form would squat before their door, to shove a
bowl of cold, slimy gruel into their reach.

Neither Diodric nor the girl would eat of the
disgusting mess, although hunger gnawed at them
terribly. For there were lumps of meat in the vile
gruel and Diodric dared not conjecture from what
source the Troglodytes procured their meats.

In the second day of their captivity, as nearly as
it was possible for them to tell of the passage of
time in this dark place far from the sight of the
sun, there came a change. A mewling mob of
Troglodytes paused before their cell. A huge key
was fitted into the rust-eaten lock and the door
was swung open. Dozens of strong hands caught at
them before Diodric could make a move to attack
them. Their arms were twisted behind their backs

and secured with many twistings of leathern thongs, and they were shoved forward down a passageway.

At length they emerged into a vast and dimly-lit hall. The vaulted ceiling, which was like that of some primitive and colossal cathedral, was lost in sooty grime and thick shadows.

The rough, uneven floor of this natural court was pitted at wide intervals with enormous craters. It would seem that these craters led to volcanic abysses below, for sheets of leaping flame danced above them, and painted the stony walls with rich orange tapestries of light, sending shadows vast and monstrous flickering across the stone surface.

There was a huge boulder set against one end of this colossal hall, and toward this they were thrust. Hands struck them in the back, rudely propelling them forward. They went stumbling over the rough floor, which was strewn with broken bits of stone and matted with indescribable filth. Here and there, a naked white bone or the cracked rondure of a skull could be glimpsed protruding from the fetid garbage wherewith the cavern floor was heaped. Diodric did not doubt but that these were human bones.

The upper half of the great round boulder was cut into the crude likeness of a massive throne. And seated thereon was the master of the Troglodytes, whose name, Diodric gathered, was Ningg. He had always understood the Troglodytes had sunken too far down the ladder of evolution to any longer possess the divine gift of human speech.

But it would seem that certain of them could, however haltingly, converse.

This Ningg was huge for a Troglodyte: his arms were immense with swelling thews, and his chest was as broad as a buckler. Under the shaggy tangle of his greasy mane, which was matted with filth, his little red eyes gleamed cold and malignant as the eyes of cunning serpents.

He was gross, this Ningg, with a great swollen paunch and sagging jowls that wobbled and swung with every motion of his head. Yellow tusks lifted above his sagging lower lip like fangs. Throned atop the boulder he sprawled, a vast repellent mass of obesity, leering at the girl and mumbling to his chieftains, who squatted in the filth about the throne. It would seem that the subterranean monarch had expressed a desire to look upon his captives, for he exchanged no words with them, merely running cold and gloating eyes carefully over their bodies.

Suddenly, Niane stifled a cry and caught Diodric's attention with a flash of frightened eyes. She nodded to one side. He followed her gaze, and saw . . . instruments of torment, hung upon the cavern wall behind the throne of Ningg.

There were hooks and pincers and burning irons and whips armed with metal hooks, and other grisly articles whose abhorrent purpose was all too obvious. Diodric felt his gorge rise within him, and he clamped his lips together until they whitened from the pressure. He felt the clammy breath of Fear on his face, and great globs of moisture stood out on his begrimed brow.

Fear. But not for himself. For the girl.

Ningg had followed his gaze. He chuckled, squatting like a gross ogre atop his great stone. He chuckled, and nodded to the tools of horror hanging on the wall, whose nameless stains gave grisly evidence of their frequent use. Then he nodded his shaggy head at certain iron spits suspended over the flaming mouths of the volcanic craters.

"Tomorrow," he grunted, leering down at the young warrior and the girl at his side.

"Tomorrow . . . first we . . . *play* . . . then we . . . *feed* . . . !"

Slumped, that night, against a corner of the cell while the Lady Niane slept, Diodric realized that there was no force in all of Atlantis that could save them from a grim death in this subterranean kingdom.

Unable to sleep, he lay staring into the darkness, waiting for the day and what it would bring.

★ 3 ★

The Book of Nephog Thoon

In the neighborhood of these mountains the Troglodytes dwelt.
—HANNO OF CARTHAGE: The *Periplus*

They have fallen below the level of human civilization, for they do not address one another by names; and when they behold the sun they curse it; and when they sleep they do not dream like men. The Troglodytes hollow out caverns which are their dwellings: they live on the flesh of snakes, and make only squeaking noises, for they are entirely devoid of intercourse by speech.
—PLINY: *Natural History*, V, vii.

i. The Dark Tower

There rose amid the foothills of the Mountains of the Terror a tall tower of dark, smooth stone. Therein the Lemurian sorcerer, Nephog Thoon, had dwelt for two hundred and nine years. In truth, he did not miss the companionship of his fellow men, for he had found those men whom he had known to be either fools, or buffoons, or oafs. He ventured but seldom from his lonely tower, and was content in the main to devote himself to those intriguing studies which are at once the solace of the loneliness of wizards, and the source of their uncanny and other-worldly wisdom, whereon their strange arts are founded.

In his person, the magister was a true Lemurian of unmixed and very ancient blood. He was tall and lean and sour-faced; bald, his round yellow skull wore a black velvet cap to keep away the night damps and chills. His visage was cadaverous and bony, with a long nose, a keen and alert and suspicious pair of black eyes, slightly slanted; and his jaw wore a long beard dyed green, which was a source of great pride and care to him. For the rest, his skin was yellow as a lemon, wrinkled and seamed with his centuries, and his gaunt body was spry and bony.

The old Lemurian sorcerer shared these mountains with the vile and repulsive breed of the Troglodytes who infested in great numbers the caverns beneath the roots of these mountains. With such repellent and dwarfish folk he held no traffic whatever, and had long since set up pillars of gray rock at intervals about his groves and gardens (in the midst of which his tower rose) whereon were engraven certain glyphs and talismans of considerable potency which the Troglodytes did not like to look upon. Indeed, they could not be dragged by force squealing into the proximity of these nameless and terrible symbols. Thus the hermit-like old sorcerer was not disturbed by the proximity of his repugnant and loathsome neighbors.

The bottom story of his tower was, as is the custom of magicians, given over to his Seat of Power: it was all one circular chamber walled with stone, the inner walls thereof hung from floor to ceiling with tapestries of olden work. In the center of the stone floor rose a dais of twelve steps, and each step was fashioned from a different metal: the

lowest step was of brown iron; then came steps of
bronze, brass, copper and the metal the Atlanteans
called *kassiteros;* and there were other steps
sheathed in lead, silver, gold, orichalc, platinum,
electrum, and the rare Lemurian metal, jazite,
whose glittering surface flashed with changeful
and fluid hues like a surface of shimmering opal.

Set or graven into these steps of the Twelve
Metals were all manner of runes and glyphs and
pictograms, and sigils and amulets and talismans
of curious force, some of which glowed lumi-
nously with the radiance of their own Power.

Atop this twelve-stepped dais rose a thronechair
of ancient wood that was black with age. Seated
thereon, Nephog Thoon was robed and invested
with Power; throned among the symbols of his
magistry, he was the center of a web of mysterious
forces and alignments, influences and tensions,
connections and lines of force. Throned and invested at the Pole of his Power, he could peer into
the distant vistas of past or of future ages, and
perceive, if but dimly, the shape of things to come
and the shadowy forms of things that once were.

The upper chambers of his tower were given
over to strange and mystical purposes. One chamber was walled with shelves of sleek crimson wood,
whereupon stood all manner of strange and rare
and curious books. Some of these were bound in
leather or in the skin of beasts or the hide of dragons; others were bound between plates of rare and
precious metals, carven ivory, or odd woods. There

were rolls of parchment and vellum scrolls, and certain texts of an incredible antiquity which were incised upon tablets of clay or of stone. This was the librarium of the old sorcerer, and it held many rare literary treasures, among these a copy of that most ancient and fabulous document, the *Lemurian Chronicles,* whose sheets were thin foil of an imperishable and nameless metal. There were at this point of time only two other copies of the *Lemurian Chronicles* known to exist over all of the earth, and one of these was in the archives of the great Temple of Pazadon, Lord of the Sea, in the City of the Golden Gates; and the other lay in certain secret vaults in the city of Sait-ya in the land of Khem-Mu (which we know as Egypt).

A higher story of the tower was given over to the chemical mysteries, and here Nephog Thoon had his laboratorium. Long tables of steel and porcelain were set along the walls, and they bore all manner of earthenware jars and pots and vases, and objects of ceramic, glass and porcelain, and the various instruments of the chemical arts; such as crucibles and athanors, aludels and cucurbits, and others of unknown purpose for which I have no name.

Herein, with many long and tedious experimentations, the old Lemurian sorcerer sought to fix the quicksilver, to create *aqua viva,* to isolate the Prima Materia, to distill the *theion hudor* or Divine Water, and to perfect the transmutation of the baser into the nobler metals.

Against the far wall of this chamber rose a mighty alembic of glazed stone, and a tall slender *kerotakis* of glistening copper.

Another chamber on this story was draped in black velvet and bore only a huge chair, before which stood a massive Speculum, or Wizard's Mirror, of black and shining steel, wherein whose polished and darksome surface Nephog Thoon was wont to converse with and behold the spirits of the dead philosophers and sages, and to communicate with certain crystalloid intelligences which dwelt in the inner chambers of the Moon, and with a certain fungoid entity which inhabited the ninth moon of Saturn.

The uppermost story of the tower contained the personal apartments of the old sorcerer, and there he slept in a great bed of somber and funereal purples, or, betimes, observed the planets and the constellations of the Zodiac through a mighty lens of curved and polished crystal.

Such was the tower wherein dwelt the sorcerer Nephog Thoon. I describe it to you in this place, because we shall not again visit it until the ending of my tale.

ii. The Garden of Magic

Nephog Thoon had arisen with the first light of
dawn in a vile and vicious temper. The night before it had been his intent to make certain astrologic observations and measurements of the star
which the Atlanteans knew by the name Sfanomoë,
but which we of today call the planet Venus. But
much to the disgruntlement and annoyance of the
old sorcerer, the heavens had been obscured by a
black vapor for much the greater part of the night,
and only the red and evil spark of the star Azphar
had been visible.

He rose, thus, in a vile mood, and broke his fast
with black olives, yellow cheese, brown bread, and
red wine. Finishing his simple repast, he retired
grumbling to his garden wherein he grew many
small magics. There were planted in this garden a
curious variety of herbs and flowers and cacti and
fungi from which he extracted certain essential
oils, pollens, juices, and powders which were use-
ful to his science. But this morn a blight was on
the fungi and dew lay thick on the leaves of the
cacti and he could grub up from the earth only a
ripe mandrake or two, and these with certain difficulty, as the hairy, repulsive, and man-shapen

roots clung squealing to the earth, snapped at his fingers with tiny thornlike teeth, and glared furiously at him with little red eyes like crumbs of ruby.

Snatching the wriggling roots from the soil, he thrust them squeaking into a sack at his waist, and paused to regain his breath.

Then it was that Nephog Thoon, squinting against the morning sun, perceived that he was about to have a visitor. For on the slopes of the hill whereon he had his tower, grove, and garden, he saw, still some distance off, the figure of a man in gray robes, toiling up the steep incline.

The old Lemurian squinted his sharp black eyes, striving to make out the features of this unwanted visitor, but this he could not do as the person had drawn the cowl of his hooded robes about his face so that his features could not be seen. But he was a human, and no Troglodyte or Rmoahal, that much was certain.

The Lemurian continued to contemplate the visitor as he made his slow, laborious way up the slope of the hill. He observed that the fellow aided his climb with a tall staff of dark wood. Nephog Thoon was conscious of an internal unease: he did not like the precise shade of the person's gray cloak, and he heartily distrusted the configuration of that tall and seemingly innocuous staff. And he felt an inkling of the identity of his visitor, and a premonition of discomfiture to come, and he groaned slightly and cursed under his breath.

The man in the hooded gray robe toiled up the slope until he stood gazing at the sorcerer. He stood just beyond the row of inscribed pillars that formed a magical barrier against the filthy Troglodytes. But the signs on that pillared row also gave warning to another class of visitor besides the swarming and dwarfish Dwellers in the Depths.

The gray-robed stranger stood watching Nephog Thoon as he stood amidst the neat rows of his magical garden: and the old Lemurian was suddenly conscious of his grubby hands, of the loamy stains on the knees of his patched robe, and that a smudge of black soil had somehow come to mark his sallow and wrinkled cheek.

When he saw that Nephog Thoon was not going to be the first to speak, the gray stranger raised his hand in greeting and called out:

"Good time of day unto you, friend! That is a fine garden you have there. May I, of your courtesy, have permission to cross your Barrier? For I would have converse with you on a certain subject; indeed, I have come far for the privilege of conversing with you."

And as he spoke he traced a curious sign on the air with the forefinger of his right hand. A *very* curious sign, indeed: for it hung on the air for some moments, a tracery of dim blue fire, until it expired and faded from view in a small explosion of sparks.

Nephog Thoon gave an inward groan: his worst premonitions were realized; however, there was no recourse. So, tracing the same symbol on the air in a tangle of blue flame, he sourly bade the gray stranger to enter into his demesne.

He had been right, then. The gray robe was that of the Thaumaturgae, and the staff of dark inscribed wood was the Staff of a brother magician.

He had a feeling he was really in for something this time. But there was nothing to do but welcome the Thaumaturge to his tower and listen to the message that had thus been brought to him from his brother magicians.

iii. The Quest of Kynaethon

There stood against the wall of the tower a low bench of wood, whereon now the old Lemurian invited his guest to seat himself and rest his legs, which doubtless were weary from traveling. Also, he summoned, by touching his forefinger to one of the talismanic seal rings which adorned his long and bony fingers, a certain Air elemental, by name Szaliel, which was obedient to his commands. This Being he bade bring cold water, a cup of wine, and fresh fruit for the pleasure and refreshment of his fellow sorcerer.

The other, seating himself with a grateful sigh on the bench, threw back his gray hood and leaned

his staff against the side of the tower. Thus un-
cowled, he revealed a youngish face, as wizards go:
he was scarcely over one hundred years, and had
the fresh boyish face of immaturity (for magicians,
whose lives are longer by centuries than the lives
of men, are wont to age more slowly than mortals).

The invisible spirit of the Air whisked a tray of
refreshments before the nose of the visitor, who accepted the cup, mixed wine with the cold water,
and drank it thirstily, while selecting a plump and
juicy fruit plucked an instant before from a secret
garden in the wastes of primal and unknown
Cathay, where as yet the race of man had not
penetrated.

"And what have the Thaumaturgae to do with
old Nephog Thoon?" the sorcerer demanded tes-
tily. "I attend not your coventicles; I have naught
to do with your secrets and your councils; I wish
only to be left alone to pursue the Nine Sciences
at my leisure."

The younger magician gave him a frank, quiz-
zical glance.

" 'Naught to do'?" he repeated. " 'Naught to do'
with your brother devotees of the Secret Sciences?
Ah, good Master Nephog Thoon, you are too mod-
est. Your brethren speak most highly of the extent
and depth of your learning, of your most respectful age and seniority, of your accomplishments,
which are reputed both ingenious and without
flaw!"

Before such flattering words from a colleague,

albeit a junior, the old Lemurian's stiff and suspicious air thawed almost visibly. "Tush!" he admonished weakly, and: "Oh, now."

"But let me make myself known to you," the other went on in a rambling and discursive tone. "I am hight the magister Kynaethon of Kernê, and at your service, elder brother! It is true that our Senior brethren have dispatched me hither for a most weighty and momentous purpose, for dark times are come upon Atlantis and great dangers threaten the equilibrium of the cosmic forces wherewith we work our arts." The words of young Kynaethon had taken on, by now, a more somber and serious coloring. "Indeed, if the power of the Dragon triumphs over The Light, all of this land will be thrust deep into a perdurable and everlasting darkness."

The old sorcerer eyed him sourly. "And what have these matters to do with old Nephog Thoon, sirrah? I have naught to do with the world and its ways, as I have made plain time and again."

The younger magician smiled at him sunnily.

"Long and arduous hath been my quest to find your tower, elder brother! For great and portentous deeds are in the offing, and a mighty mission requires the aid of an elder Thaumaturgist of tact, delicacy, tenacity, and wisdom: in a word, of just such a revered Karcist as yourself."

"I feared it would be something like that," Naphog Thoon said, grumblingly. "Well, get on with it, boy!"

And Kynaethon bent close until his lips were very near the ears of old Nephog Thoon. And he began whispering urgently, but in so low a tone that none could hear, even had any been present. At great length his communications continued, and from time to time he gestured, either a lift of appealing hands, or a vehement, slashing motion with the flat of the hand; and to these whispered words the old Lemurian responded by closing his eyes from time to time, or permitting a slight shudder to shake his bony shoulders. At one point he rolled up his eyes as if to say "What more?"; and he muttered once, in a glum tone, the phrase: "I knew it!"; and at another point he uttered a doleful groan.

Thus was the Word of the Thaumaturgae passed to Nephog Thoon the Lemurian, and thus was the long quest of Kynaethon accomplished in the passing-on of this message. And thus were deeds and events of enormous and millennial importance set into motion, and through these would the world be changed and all of future time be other than it now tended.

iv. The Departure

When he was done, Kynaethon bade the old Lemurian an affable but abrupt farewell, and strode off down the sloping hillside once again, to be about his own and his Masters' business in the great world. For a long time, Nephog Thoon sat glumly on the bench, deep in his own thoughts.

At length he roused himself and entered his tower by the great arched doorway of gray stone.

This doorway was overgrown with curious green roses which were trained about the portal by means of a trelliswork of wooden slats. Very curious indeed were these roses, for as the old Lemurian stumped past the threshold, they turned slightly on their stalks as if to observe him; and, in sooth, these most unusual blossoms bore each within its center something small and bright and jellied that had a most remarkable resemblance to an human eye. The bright, inquisitive scrutiny of the green roses turned upon Nephog Thoon as he passed within the tower, and had it been any other than he (for the roses were trained to recognize their master), they would have set up a small shrill clamor of alarm.

The old sorcerer was in a vile mood, and he turned to snarl a rude query at the inquisitive, but inoffensive, blossoms.

"What are you fools staring at?" he snarled, as he clumped within.

Satisfied with the identity of the tall gaunt figure, the optically-gifted roses turned stiffly again to face outward, continuing their vegetable vigilance.

Within the tower, Nephog Thoon, grumbling

and muttering under his breath, rummaged
through sacks and casks, barrels and chests, cup-
boards and closets, selecting a variety of oddments
which he then stuffed into a sack. From a rack of
tall staves, which differed each from the other by
minute gradations of coloring, height, weights,
and configuration, he selected a tall black staff of
polished ebony, set with small rows of hieroglyphic
characters picked out in bright gold. From a brass-
bound chest he selected a most curious cloak. The
cloak was lined with a stiff glassy fabric on its
underside, a silken stuff that was oddly most difficult to see, for the eye wrenched aside of its own
accord and the gaze slid off the glassy surface like
droplets of water from waxed cloth.

On its outer surface, the cloak was deep and soft
and dark as midnight. Many magics had been
worked over this wizard's cloak. Among its rustling and enigmatic folds lurked the smell of
meteors and the odor of thunderbolts.

The sorcerer then visited his laboratorium on
the floors above. Here many experimentations
were in various stages of progress. Some of these
would have to be discontinued and postponed, but
certain others could be left under the supervision
of the Air elemental Szaliel, whom Nephog Thoon
at once summoned and lectured sternly and at
length. Szaliel, like all his aerial and insubstantial
kind, was amiable and not unintelligent, but of a
flighty and unserious character, and the sorcerer
was forced to threaten certain frightening and

transmundane punishments should the invisible
Being falter in his loyalty or neglect the various
duties that were now imposed upon him.

But at length all was in readiness, and the old
sorcerer left his tower, sealing the door behind him
with potent sigils of magic, and, after issuing certain final commandments to the guardian roses in
a tone of voice pitched too high for any but the
sensitive vegetable ear to comprehend, he went
grumpily off among the winding hills upon the
mission thus imposed upon him by the Thaumaturgae, the worldwide brotherhood of magicians
to which fraternity he indeed belonged, as did all
other Karcists of the earth, save and excepting only
those followers of the Black Arts sworn to the service of Chaos and Its son, Thelatha the Dragon.

It would be to little purpose were I to describe
in detail the paths by which the old Lemurian
sorcerer penetrated deeply into the Mountains of
the Terror. Indeed, not all of these paths are
capable of description save in the Secret Language of Magicians, for certain of the roads
Nephog Thoon followed are not of this world at
all, and took him, in what might not inaccurately
be described as shortcuts, through transmundane
regions and planes of existence which magicians
call "The Halfworld," a place which lies out of
space and time, between the World of Men and the
Otherworld of Shadows. But of such matters it is
unwise to speak openly, for although I, the Author
of this History, am not bound by the oaths of se-

crecy imposed by the Thaumaturgae, I am nonetheless vulnerable to their vengeance.

Suffice it to relate that, in a remarkably brief
time (as *this* world measures time), the sorcerer
came by secret paths into the subterranean regions
of Ningg, the Lord of the Troglodytes, although
none of that vile and scrambling horde was aware
of the trespass.

The old sorcerer traced his way through the
labyrinthine passages of the underground domain
without the slightest difficulty or hesitation, although never before in the two hundred and nine
years of his existence in this incarnation had he
had occasion to venture thus into the depths beneath these unwholesome and ill-reputed mountains. He followed the swiftest and the shortest
paths possible to the cells where Diodric and the
Lady Niane lay imprisoned. The means by which
Nephog Thoon accomplished this feat may be of
some interest to my reader, if only for the light
thus thrown upon the sorcerous arts.

v. The Third Eye of Nephog Thoon

It seems that every human being presently car-
nate on this plane of being—which is known as the
Physical, for reasons which are obvious—possesses

a counterpart or duplicate body on the next plane, which is the Astral.

This Astral body is very different from the Physical body, just as the two planes differ greatly. In brief, the Astral body resembles a thick-based and tapering cone of vibrant light, with a radiant and fiery Core.

In this Astral body are certain organs, seven in number, which are known by the Lemurian word, *Chakra*. One of these Chakras is located near the crest of the flamelike Astral body: if the Astral and the Physical bodies of a human being were superimposed, it could be seen that this particular Chakra is located in the forehead, just above and exactly between the two eyes of the human body, but at a certain slight depth within the skull, approximately in the location of a small and now-insignificant gland of little value, use or importance, called the *pineal*.

I speak in the present tense, of course: but my story is laid at the close of the Second Age of Atlantis, many tens of thousands of years ago. In the golden age of Lemuria, hundreds of thousands of years before Atlantis, this pineal gland was more active, and the Chakra which was its Astral equivalent—the famous "Third Eye" of occult science —was in more frequent use. Every magician, sorcerer, wizard, and thaumaturge could command the use of this organ as Astral vision, together with many priests, seers, and prophets. Intervening ages, and the forces of evolution, have robbed us of this rare sense; even in the ancient days of Atlantis (as the verses quoted in my Prologue from the *Book of Dzyan* state), those men capable of Astral vision were very few; and Nephog Thoon was one of them. Today, save certain sages of Tibet and the members of a Secret School located in the Hidden City of Damcar in the deserts of Arabia, mastery of the Third Eye is virtually unknown.

It was by means of this organ of vision that Nephog Thoon was able to perceive the location of the two he sought. For, while on this Physical plane many walls of dense rock stood between him and the two prisoners, the barriers of the Astral plane are less substantial and are transparent to the Third Eye; on that plane, his Astral counterpart could clearly see the throbbing radiant forms of Diodric and Niane, and by coordinating Astral positions with the Physical, he was able to locate the cell wherein the unfortunate pair lay imprisoned.

vi. The Staff of Power

When Diodric perceived a tall form suddenly rise up before the barred entrance to the cell, he feared that the time of their torment had come and he resolved to fall upon the Troglodytes the moment the door lay open, and go down fighting.

To his astonishment, however, a second glance informed him that the gaunt cloaked figure before their cell was too tall to be a Troglodyte; indeed, it would have taken two of the squat, repulsive little monsters, standing one upon the shoulders of the other, to achieve the stature of Nephog Thoon—for, of course, it was he who stood at the entrance to Diodric's cell.

His astonishment increased measurably as the old sorcerer, grunting slightly as if from the twinge of an arthritic pain in his ancient joints, bent over to whisper a potent and terrific Word into the earlike opening of the lock—which, upon the instant, obediently unlocked itself.

"Come! Swiftly, now. I am here to help you escape," the unknown stranger said sharply as the door opened itself. A thousand questions tumbled through Diodric's brain, but he did not bother wasting time to ask them. Instead, seizing the pale, frightened girl, he thrust her forward and followed her from the cell.

The old sorcerer examined the two mortals with sharp eyes—eyes, I should add, which perceptibly softened as he observed the sorry conditions of the stalwart young warrior and the pitiable, frightened face of the wan young woman. For, although Nephog Thoon deeply and bitterly resented the intrusion upon his leisure studies which this mission entailed, he was not without a heart, nor was he incapable of feeling sympathy for the abused.

Diodric peered through the dim light at the tall, gaunt figure which had so unexpectedly loomed up out of nowhere, like a ghostly apparition.

"Who are you?" he demanded.

"A friend!" the Lemurian grunted. "We have no time to talk now. This way—and quickly. I have laid a small spell on the Troglodytes, but, alas, one of brief duration. They will be on our track in no time, for the disgusting brutes can sniff out our trail like wolves. Hurry! There will be time for explanations later!"

Diodric could see the sense of the stranger's words. And, whether this was a trick or not, mattered very little. They could hardly find themselves in worse trouble than they were already in, and any change must therefore be a change for the better. Hence he wasted no time in hurrying after the old sorcerer, who was already stalking swiftly off down the gloomy passage without as much as a backward glance. Taking the arm of Niane and helping her over the rough and poorly lit floor of the cavern, he pursued the swiftly receding figure.

Without even the slightest difficulty or hesitation, the old Lemurian sorcerer retraced his path through the black labyrinth of subterranean passageways at a remarkable speed.

And although both the Throne warrior and the Lady Niane were greatly weakened and fatigued by the harsh treatment they had received during their imprisonment, the chance for escape thus offered them so lifted their spirits and revitalized them, that they found it not difficult to keep pace with the long legs of Nephog Thoon.

In an amazingly short time they had left the warrens of the Troglodytes far behind and were rapidly ascending toward the surface of the earth by means of certain paths which were known only to the occult eye of Nephog Thoon. He would very much have liked to utilize, on this return journey, those uncanny shortcuts through the Halfworld which had made his original journey so much more brief. But there were Things in the Halfworld it is not wholly safe to look upon, and there are Shapes and Forces there which tempt the soul and shake the reason of those who venture unprepared into the World That Lies Between The Worlds. Alas, since neither Diodric nor the Lady Niane were Initiates in the Mysteries, he wisely deemed it unsafe to expose them to the shadowy perils of that occult realm. Hence he was forced to take a longer route, which gave increase to the dangers of discovery.

And, in sooth, they had not ventured very far along these paths when his keen old ears caught the distant, howling cry of enraged Troglodytic voices. The spell that he had cast over the denizens of the depths was of brief duration: already the escape of the captives had been discovered, and now the pittering little horde was yelping on their trail like so many hounds.

But there was naught he could do about this, but to hurry forward. And hurry he did.

At times the howling faded, as if the loathsome horde that seethed through the tunnels behind them had momently lost their trail; but, always, it rose on their tracks again.

From time to time the old Lemurian called upon the queer resources of the great, black Staff he carried. One passage through which they fled was blocked by the colossal spiderwebs Diodric had noticed when first the Troglodytes had brought him down into these tunnels. These webs Nephog Thoon eliminated in a manner that eluded precise definition: he would raise his ebony Staff before him and it would flare with a momentary, eye-searing brilliance; whereupon the webs would shrivel, smoking, as if from a flash of intolerable fire. The curious thing about all this was that Diodric was not conscious of any sensation of heat.

But the uses to which the old Lemurian sorcerer put his mighty Staff were few, for each employment drained the Staff of a small increment of its Power; thus he grudged the use thereof, save in such extremities of need where any other recourse was futile or impossible.

vii. The Abyss of the Worm

They came, with some passage of time, to that tremendous pit wherever a bridge of natural stone arched above vertiginous deeps. Diodric remembered how the Troglodytes had borne himself and the Lady Niane across this giddy way; and he recalled, with what inward shudderings I give my reader leave to imagine for himself, the loathsome and terrific Worm that lay coiled in its fetid nest at the bottom of this gulf.

And it was here, as fate would have it, that the pursuing and clamorous horde of the Troglodytes caught up with them.

They had traversed about one-third of the span of this stone arch. The rocky surface was slippery with slime, and nauseating and gelid winds blew from the shadowy depths below to tug at their hair and garments, troubling their balance. They could only progress slowly and with much care, for the footing was unsound. And here the yowling mob encountered them. It swept from the black mouth of the tunnel wherethrough they had emerged but a moment before. Seeing their quarry before them on the bridge, the throng of Troglodytes gave voice to the most blood-curdling shriek of gloating and malicious joy. Then the agile little monsters were after them, and moving much more rapidly than they could go.

However, they continued to inch their way across the narrow arch of slippery stone, Diodric carrying the Lady Niane, who found the vertiginous gulf to either side most discomposing.

"Hurry, lad!" the old sorcerer implored from behind him. "Get yourself and the lass to safety on the other side."

"What of yourself?" demanded Diodric. The old Lemurian cackled with nasty amusement.

"I have a certain little trick to show our diminutive friends," he sniggered. "It will take but a moment; however, you must reach the safety of the further ledge before I can employ it. Faster, faster!"

Sweat streamed down the young warrior's face. Salt droplets blurred his smarting eyes. Yet he went forward over the bridge with every bit of speed he could achieve. His sandals were beslimed with the foulness of the caverns wherethrough they had come: his footing was slippery and most insecure; the slightest false step would precipitate the girl and himself into the shadowy abyss that yawned below—into the hideous jaws of that mindless and colossal Worm that slept in the bottom of the pit!

Hardly daring to breathe, he inched his precarious way along. Step by step, foot by foot, yard by yard. The bridge seemed to continue on forever. And, with every slow moment of time that went ticking by, the yammering and exultant roar of the Troglodytes sounded nearer—*nearer*.

After an infinity, he staggered from the bridge and stood in relative safety on the narrow, sloping ledge. He set the girl down with a groan of relief, and turned to look at their mysterious companion.

Nephog Thoon stood partway out on the bridge, over which the swarming Troglodytes had now come more than halfway.

The tall Lemurian stood calm and serene as if unaware of danger. He surveyed the snarling faces of the advancing swarm with a placid and un-worried gaze. They were so close that he could see the cold, red glint of their venomous, squinting eyes and the moisture that glistened on their bared tusks and the greenish froth that foamed and bubbled at the corners of their slathering jaws. Almost, they were within reach of him; almost— but not quite. There must have been ninety or a full hundred of them already upon the bridge; and there were hundreds more that boiled from the black cavern mouth like angry bees from a dis-turbed nest.

Just as the working claws of the foremost Trog-lodyte were about to clutch at the hem of his cloak, the old sorcerer suddenly lifted his great black Staff above his head.

It blazed with a terrific light! Blue-white, like the fires of lightning bolts, was that terrible and searing radiance.

A scream of panic and pain tore from the many-throated throng. Bred in the crawling dark-ness of this subterranean realm, seldom if ever exposed to the brilliance of day, the slitted, scarlet eyes of the deformed little monsters could not endure such terrible radiance.

But very swiftly, then, before the blinded and panic-stricken little dwarfs could scramble off the bridge and escape, the sorcerer brought the butt of his Staff down sharply. It rang against the stone arch of the bridge with a deafening crash of thunder.

And the bridge—broke.

There was a deep, bass rumble of grating stone. A sharp, splintering crack sang through the dim, echoing air. And the stone bridge broke off sharply, just inches before the place where Nephog Thoon was standing.

With a slow, gathering thunder, tons of shattered stone and scores of squealing, wriggling Troglodytes fell into the abyss.

Dozens of other Troglodytes were swept into the chasm as well, when the stub of the bridge snapped off at the further end, dragging down with it the narrow, stone shelf of the ledge whereon they stood.

The air was filled with thunder, as from a tremendous avalanche. The screeching cries of the falling, the maimed, the doomed, were not in the least human. Dust came whirling up from the depths below, and shrouded the tall figure of the old Lemurian thaumaturge in boiling clouds.

Then it was over. Nor were they any longer pursued.

viii. Safety!

It was not long after this that the dusty and bone-tired adventurers again gained the mountain peak. Seldom had Diodric encountered so welcome a sight as that which now met his eyes, the sleek, glittering ovoid of their *viwân* still tethered to the rock spear.

He was almost at the limits of his strength, but he lifted the half-fainting girl over the deck and clambered after her. He noticed, without really paying much attention to the fact, that she staggered into the cabin without a moment's pause, and found the bundle of her belongings still intact, lying in a corner of the cabin where her captors had negligently thrown it days earlier. And he did not see, nor would he have understood, the look of tremendous relief that went over her features as she dug her trembling fingers within the depths of the bundle—and found *That* for whose safety she so greatly had feared.

The old sorcerer lingered on the mountain peak, his eyes caressing the ancient Lemurian airboat with worshipful admiration. He was minded, seeing the splendid craft, of the mighty achievements of the long-vanished people from whom he was descended, and of the greatness of that first and most glorious of the human civilizations of this globe.

His eyes were misted and thoughtful. He stroked gently with his fingers the glistening metal of the hull. "Ah! So, so," he muttered half to himself, absently.

We shall leave him alone with his memories, for a little.

It was late afternoon, an hour or two later. Diodric, scrambling among the gneiss scarps of the mountain peak, had been so fortunate as to discover a mountain spring. There was no telling what colossal subterranean pressures had been so powerful as to force a stream of water to this extreme height; however, he did not question their good fortune. He called the others. They drank long and thirstily of the clear, pure, and intensely cold waters, and the young warrior and the girl were heartily pleased to lave their filthy, bruised, and weary limbs in the sparkling fountain. As the old sorcerer had been foreminded enough to fetch from his tower a flask of the heady black wine of old Pythondus, green cheese, succulent dates, and coarse black bread, together with a packet of dried meat wrapped in waxed paper, they were able to assuage their gnawing hunger as well as sate their thirst.

As the exhausted pair sprawled on the soft bunks of the airboat cabin, munching the delicious repast, the old Lemurian took this advantage to explain his presence.

"I am the Magister Nephog Thoon, a sorcerer of no small repute," he began expansively. "I dwell in a tower situated in the foothills of these mountains, and by my magic arts I perceived the descent of your remarkable aerial boat as well as your capture by the despicable and degenerate little beastlings who infest the bowels of these mountains. While it is my accustomed wont to dwell apart from the habitations of my fellow-men, I am not insensible of the pleasures of human companionship, and from time to time I weary of the discourse of spirits and long for the voice of man. It is, moreover, my habit to undertake a deed of mercy, kindness, or altruism at least once a century—if only for the health of my soul."

At this, he smirked a little, in a self-satisfied manner. And Niane smiled. She found the querulous and aged man amusing; and her gratitude for his timely intervention into their perils was limitless. Speaking up hesitantly, she said as much.

"Tush, girl!" the old fellow said, blushing a little at the warmth of her words and averting his keen old eyes reluctantly from the generous glimpses of her maiden flesh rendered visible by the sorry condition of her gown.

He went on in an amiable tone, explaining that he could hardly sit idly by while the degenerate vermin of the Underways worked their vicious torments on the bodies of helpless captives. And,

he said, so pleasant did he find their companionship, that it had come into his mind to accompany
them, at least until they were free of these mountains, if they would permit a third to join their
party.

Thereupon commenced some discussion of the
future: Niane had understood that the Royal party
would attempt to reach distant Trysadon, which,
being the westernmost of the Ten Cities of Atlantis, would afford the exiles a refuge of the
greatest possible safety. But Diodric disagreed: he
doubted that the White Emperor would flee to
the utmost extremities of the island continent; be-
lieving the Divine Pnomphis reluctant to waste a
single day before attempting to seize the City of the
Golden Gates from the Dragon. It was his assumption that the Royal party would go no further than
the city of Caiphul, on the shores of the river
Nomis. Caiphul, he argued, which was the most
ancient of the Atlantean cities, and which had been
the capital of the First Empire, and which had
mastered tremendous heights of scientific weaponry
in the great, golden days of Zailm Numinos, might
still preserve many of the antique instruments of
war whose technology had long since been lost.
Would not the Emperor, in his fierce thirst for
revenge, seek to achieve this haven, there perchance to augment his forces with the mysterious
armaments of the Lemurians?

At length the dispute ended. It was decided that
on the morrow they would undertake a flight to the

ancient city of Caiphul, on the river Nomis; from thence, if the Emperor proved not to have made Caiphul the destination of his journey, they could proceed in the direction of westernmost Trysadon. Surely, at some point along this western route, they would encounter the Imperial party, or learn more precise news as to its whereabouts.

And, as to the proposal by Nephog Thoon that he accompany them on their quest, the two youthful Atlanteans gave unquestioned and enthusiastic assent.

They slept that night in the airboat, fearless of any further trouble from the Troglodytes upon the assurance of the Lemurian that Ningg would not touch them again. The two young people slept like the dead, so great was their fatigue and the extent of the nervous strain whereunder they had suffered during the days of their captivity. Only Nephog Thoon found it difficult to sleep. He prowled about the deck of the *viwân,* muttering to himself, peering at the sky, in a bad and sour humor with himself.

For it troubled the old man that he had been forced to utter lies to the two youngsters.

Alas, these were but the first of the many lies he would have to tell them.

★ 4 ★

The Book of Gryphax

Through their scientific attainments during this culmination of Atlantean civilization, the most intellectual and energetic members of the race gradually obtained more and more insight into the working of Nature's laws, and more and more control over her hidden forces. The desecration of this knowledge and its use for selfish ends is what constitutes sorcery. The awful effects of such desecration are well enough exemplified in the terrible catastrophes that overtook the race. For when once the black practice was inaugurated it was destined to spread in ever-widening circles.

The battle of Armageddon is fought over and over again in every age of the world's history.

—W. Scott-Elliot: *Atlantis and the Lost Lemuria,* (edition of 1954, p. 29)

i. The Rising of Polinax

The sun god rose slowly over the edges of the
world, and flooded Atlantis with his golden rays.

The travelers rose early. They had slept deep
and sound, and young bodies soon recover from
even the most exhausting extremities of fatigue.
Diodric and the Lady Niane were eager to be gone
from these dark and unpleasantly inhabited mountains. As well, the old Lemurian sorcerer was
happy to be off. Thus, after a hasty breaking of
their fast on the remnants of last night's meal, the
Throne warrior severed the last of the leathern
thongs wherewith the Troglodytes had bound the
airboat to the mountain ledge, and the *viwân*
ascended into the clear, bright morning sky.

The old sorcerer took upon himself the role of
navigator. With many learned allusions to authori-
tative texts, such as the works of the ancient

Atlantean geographer Orcys, he directed Diodric
to assume a course to the west and slightly north.
The flying craft wove for a time through vertiginous chasms and between sheer walls of cliffy
stone, since it could ascend to no greater height
than this; but, in an hour or so, the Mountains of
the Terror fell away into foothills which themselves, with some little time, yielded to a forested
landscape of rolling meadows, laced with small
silver ribbons that were rivers.

The old sorcerer was fascinated with the sensation of flight. This achievement of the ancient
Lemurian scientists engaged his lively and analyt-
ical intelligence, which was of considerable depth
and profundity: a magician being, of course, very
much akin to a scientist in his picturing of the
Cosmic All as a system wherein an equilibrium
of forces was maintained through a series of inter-
locking and immutable natural laws. He could
not help reflecting on the enormous loss to mankind which had come about with the gradual sub-
mergence of the Lemurian continent ages ago.
The Lemurians had achieved an astounding knowledge and mastery of the Laws of the Physical
Plane. But when their unstable and volcanic continent had broken up, although most of the populace had escaped the resultant deluge by means
of a gigantic aerial navy of *viwâns* such as the one
in which he now rode, vast archives and labora-
toriums of scientific wisdom had been irretriev-
ably lost—and the knowledge continued to dwin-
dle from millennium to millennium, as rare books

crumbled or were destroyed. For a time, under the First, or Lemurian, Dynasty of glittering Caiphul, a technological renaissance had brought science to new golden heights; but the collapse of that Dynasty and the dark ages that followed before the rise of the City of the Golden Gates, had robbed the Atlanteans of much that they had so slowly and painfully re-won from the wreckage of the past.

They passed over a land of dense forests while Polinax the Sunlord rose toward the zenith of the heavens. Niane stifled a small cry, and called the attention of her companions to a number of amazing monsters which slowly, in groups of a dozen or so, were emerging from the depths of the forests beneath their hurtling keel.

The beasts looked like walking hills, so vast was their bulk, and their four columnar legs were like the trunks of great trees. They were covered with dense matted hair, curling like fleece, but darker in color. A fantastic proboscis obtruded from the center of their enormous heads: the limb curled and coiled, as prehensile as a serpent; and from their jaws titanic ivory tusks curled.

The aerial travelers gazed down with curious eyes as the gigantic herd of woolly mammoths grazed in hundreds along the edges of the great central forests of Atlantis.

By midday they had left the Mountains of the

Terror far behind and were well on the way to the city of Caiphul.

The ancient Lemurian metropolis lay beyond a region of dense and tropic jungles. At their present speed—Diodric, still largely unfamiliar with the abilities and limitations of the aerial ship, dared not strain the engines to any greater velocity than that at which they were presently flying—it should take about a day and a half of steady flight to reach their destination.

So peaceful did the land below look, that it was difficult for the travelers to realize the terrible convulsion of civil war, treachery, and revolution, that had shaken the civilization of the Atlanteans to its foundation. For the grim struggle of a secret society of Black Magicians to overthrow and trample down the Divine Dynasty that had ruled all of the island continent for thousands of years left no visible marks on the green fields and rolling hillscapes over which they flew. None of the three had ever visited the great eastern continent the Atlanteans called Thuria and which we call Europe and Africa, then joined at Gibraltar, with the Mediterranean an inland sea; but the land below their keel seemed as primitive and peaceful as that placid continent which was still, by this era, very largely uninhabited by man, save at the great city-colonies of Tarshish, the City of the Silver Throne in the Gadeiric land, and Sait-ya, the City of the Sphinx, in Khem-Mu. One would think that the foot of man had never touched the virgin wilderness below them.

The scattered copses wherewith the hilltops were crowned were thickening now into forest-land again. Soon they flew over wooded areas which grew denser and more tropic. The jungles of Daitya lay beneath their keel now, and therein, half-buried amidst the foliage, the travelers espied the ruins of primal cities abandoned at the collapse of the First Empire. Stone towers lay like petrified and colossal trees; paving stones were split and tumbled aside, to make room for soaring boles. The deserted and jungle-whelmed cities below were a sad reminder of the devastation that follows in the wake of the collapse of civilizations.

Would a similar Dark Age of decay and degeneration follow the fall of their own Empire? They could not know, but Time would tell.

ii. The Eye of the Dragon

While the ancient Lemurian airboat conveyed Diodric, the Lady Niane, and Nephog Thoon the Lemurian sorcerer, farther and farther into the western provinces of Atlantis, a sinister and omnipotent eye followed their progress.

In the City of the Golden Gates, the reign of a Black Emperor had now replaced that of the White. The Great House on the Sacred Mount was

now invested by his Dragon warriors, and Thelatha himself sat in the Place of Power. But not on
the sacred throne. That had been hurled down
and broken into fragments, and in its place a
Black Throne had been erected.

The mighty Court of the Pylons lay dim and
empty in the dawn save the Demon King, who sat
brooding on his dark chair. He sat robed and
masked in green, as was his wont, and none knew
the reason thereof: whether it be some bodily de-
formity, some physical sign of his awful and unnatural Parentage, or that he sought safety in the
fact that his face went unknown amongst men.

He sat before a mighty Speculum of black crystal. Mirrored within the mystic depths of this
Wizard's Glass was the image of a glittering silvery airship. He watched as it sped away from the
peaks of the Mountains of the Terror and arrowed
into the morning sky.

It was, of course, the ancient *viwân* Diodric
and Niane had discovered moored to a tier of the
Great House—the vehicle wherewith they had
succeeded in escaping from the besieged and now-
conquered City.

The hidden eyes of Thelatha had followed their
adventures for the past three days since the fall of
the City of the Golden Gates. Long and closely
had his veiled and secret gaze studied the actions
of the girl Niane, and many times his probing
scrutiny had rested on the bundle of her possessions which she so carefully and anxiously guarded.
Behind that inscrutable and malignant gaze, a

powerful and superhuman intelligence was at work. The mind of Thelatha, which was only in certain ways comparable to a human intellect, was cold and keen, and awesome in its prodigious range and depth and knowledge. For hours it had weighed a thousand subtle factors: now it added the sum total of those factors, and drew a shrewd and cunning deduction therefrom.

Beyond the Court of the Pylons, in that great antechamber the Atlanteans knew as the Hall of a Hundred Columns, the lords and captains of the victorious Dragon Host stood in small groups, whispering amongst themselves, awaiting the will of their dread Master. A thousand and one details remained yet to be decided. The capital of Atlantis was fallen, the populace fled, the legions crushed and dispersed. But many of the Ten Cities remained loyal to the vanquished Emperor. The battle that had taken place some days ago on the Field of the Three Dead Kings (as it would be remembered in the Histories), and from which the Dragon Legions had emerged victorious, might well be but a prelude to many greater battles wherewith the ascendancy of Thelatha would be challenged in the days to come. As the princes of the Black Magicians whispered and conspired together, it seemed to them that their strange Master was permitting valuable time to pass while he remained indecisive. Now was the time to strike, before the loyal Cities could combine their hosts and march against the conquered capital. There were political and military decisions that should be taken now . . . but Thelatha remained wrapt in some secret problem, while irreplaceable hours sped away. For days now he had refused to communicate with his chieftains, studying with a curious intensity whatever images he conjured forth in his magic Speculum.

Prominent among the captains assembled in the hall was one Gryphax: a tall grizzled veteran whose cold and vicious ferocity, together with his grim tenacity and singleness of purpose, had earned him a position of power and privilege in the councils of the magicians. No Atlantean was he, but a barbarian from distant Thuria beyond the Gorgonian Sea. His rude mane, his heavy beard, his cold and bitter eyes of wintry gray, his squat and powerfully muscled torso, and his skin of coppery red, all denoted foreign birth. But there were many such as he among the followers of the Demon King, who had recruited much of his force on the Thurian continent.

Before the mighty doors which led into the sanctum of the pyloned court where Thelatha brooded before his magic mirror, a column of black marble had been set up, and upon its height was established a curious sphere of hollow steel.

Whispered converse throughout the Hall of a Hundred Columns hushed upon the instant, for a harsh, grating, and metallic voice now issued from this sphere. All present recognized that voice, which was spoke in tones subtly different from those employed in ordinary human speech, as if the throat and mouth that uttered them were not fully that of a man.

"Gryphax is summoned unto the Presence," said that cold voice. And all of the chieftains and commanders stood watching with curious and silent speculation as the Thurian strode past them and into the presence of the Demon King.

Were the overdue and vital commands about to be given? Had their demoniac Master at last shrugged off the peculiar melancholy which had seized and immobilized him ever since the entering of the City? Had he broken the spell of the ominous and prolonged fixation which had possessed him from the moment he entered the Chamber of the Hallows and found the crystal pedestal—*empty?*

iii. The Pursuit

It was an hour or two after dawn when Gryphax the Thurian rode forth from the City of the Golden Gates at the head of a full cohort of Dragon warriors. They took the west road and spurred their mounts savagely for speed. They did not ride horses, for it was still many thousands of years before the horse would be introduced into the ancient world by Scythian nomads from the steppes of Central Asia; neither did they ride such reptilian mounts as the swift-striding *kroter* or the massive and lumbering *zamph,* for these beasts had perished from the earth and become extinct with the destruction of the Lemurian continent eons before. Their mounts were a curious breed of giant wingless birds which the antique Aryan epics call *garuda,* and which resembled in many ways the ostrich or the emu, but which were larger and had beaks like colossal parrots, and brilliant plumage.

As Gryphax left the City he was pale and a sheen of sweat glistened on his brows. The Master he served was a strange and terrible being who struck awe into his followers and who ruled through power and through fear. There was something about the tall, terrible figure who went ever hidden from the eyes of men in robes of green that aroused an instinctive terror and loathing in ordinary mortals. It was perhaps akin to the all but universal revulsion most men feel in the presence of a deadly serpent. Although men of a certain nature were irresistibly drawn to the Dragon by the temptation of his stupendous power, through greed, or the lust of cruelty, or the hunger for dominion, or desire for the terrible cosmic secrets over which he held mastery, even the most degenerate and servile of his followers experienced a nervous terror and repugnance when exposed for long to his presence. And although this Gryphax was a cold and cunning man of unscrupulous nature and towering ambitions, and a strong and courageous warrior, devoid of fear and contemptuous of death, even he found his inner manhood —his innate *humanness*—recoiling in instinctive loathing and disgust from the sinister and faceless Thing that was his prince and his god.

The Master had commanded him to seek out the young Celt Diodric and to take from him a certain Object with which he and the girl his companion had escaped from the City of the Golden Gates three days before. The Master had told of the present location of the fleeing warrior and his party with precision. All three were to be captured for the torment, if possible; if not, they were certainly to be slain.

As the Thurian commander rode his swift-pacing garuda, his cold intelligence was bent on the tactical problems, which were considerable. He had heard of these ancient Lemurian airboats, and knew something of their speed. And the Throne warrior had three days' head start on him and his troops. It would seem hardly possible for mounted, but earthbound, warriors to catch up with the three travelers, who could soar through the clouds at many times the utmost speed he could wring from his war birds.

However, Diodric's party was not as distant as might be supposed. For the Throne warrior, in truth, had only a few hours' head start on the pursuing Dragon warriors: the young Turanian had fled from the palace at sundown and had flown only a few hours that night until overtaken by weariness. He had then, said The Master, moored

his weird flying boat in the mountains whereupon
he and the girl, taken prisoner by the savage
Troglodytes who infested that land, had lost much
time in captivity. They were now free and had
departed their mountaintop eyrie only an hour or
two ago, at sunrise.

These were the thoughts that ran through the
mind of Gryphax as he swept westward through
early morning with his Dragon warriors thundering at his heels. His face now was cold and grim.
He knew that even with so little a head start, the
Throne warrior would soon leave him far behind,
such was the velocity at which the *viwân* was capable of traveling—unless some sort of diversion
occurred to halt the flight of the three escaping
Imperials.

And the Dragon had promised him just such
a diversion.

Hour after hour the cohort of Dragon warriors
rode, ever further into the west. Ere long the soaring of purple mountains was perceived before
them. These were the Mountains of the Terror,
wherein Diodric and Niane had come so very close
to suffering an awful fate at the hands of the
merciless Troglodytes. Gryphax had no fear of the
ogre-chief, Ningg, or his dwarfed followers, for
there slept at his thigh in a sheath of cobra skins
stitched together with stiff silver wire a Blasting
Wand of prodigious and supernatural power, lent
him by The Master; and on a pack-garuda at the
end of the rear of his war party one of the terrible

Black Fire weapons—that same creation of Thelatha's evil science which was, in very great measure, responsible for the defeat of the Imperial
legions and the fall of the City of the Golden
Gates—was carried, carefully wrapped and ready
for use.

But the winding ways of the mountain range
ahead were labyrinthine and tortuous: much
time would be lost in threading a path through
those narrow and circuitous passes, and in their
pursuit of the fleeting airboat, time was of the es-
sence. Hence Gryphax diverted his troop through
the forest country, as The Master had commanded, and began circling the northern extremity of the Mountains of the Terror.

Some little time would be lost by going this
roundabout way, but in the end it would not matter. For the Demon King had promised to bring
down the *viwân* in such a manner as to make it
easy for the Thurian to seize its crew. Gryphax
wondered how this marvel would be accomplished.
For he had no doubt that The Master would make
good his word. When investing Thelatha with his
dark mission—his Black Crusade—to destroy the
civilizations of the earth and bring every living
human being under the Dominion of Darkness,
the Triple God of Chaos had bestowed upon him
a terrible mastery over the forces of nature, such
as no man on earth had ever held in all the mea-
sureless eons of the remote past.

iv. Dark Eyes

All morning the trim little airboat soared like a silvery, glittering bird above the central forests and plains of Atlantis. When the flaming sphere of Polinax had ascended to the height of heaven, the three travelers grew hungry. They had exhausted with their morning meal the slender store of food fetched thither by Nephog Thoon, and there was nothing to eat in the cabin, although Diodric had taken the precaution of filling the water bottles he had found stored beneath the bunks with the clear, cold waters of the mountain spring he had discovered.

The old Lemurian sorcerer became testy and quarrelsome as his hunger increased. His sarcastic remarks that he hoped his altruistic offer of service to their quest for the exiled Emperor of Atlantis was not to include the opportunity of starvation, were ignored by Diodric. The young Celt bent over the control console of the *viwân*, steadfastly refusing to land the craft so that they might chance to procure food in the jungles below. He was all too conscious of the fact that they were still dangerously close to the captured City of the Golden Gates and might still be in the proximity of scattered troops of Dragon warriors. Every hour of flight he could add to their total since the departure from the mountains gave them a greater margin of security and increased their chances of success. And he was not going to jeopardize the safety of the Lady Niane simply because of the empty belly of Nephog Thoon.

The girl was singularly silent and had been thus throughout the long hours of their flight. Many times her dark eyes rested on the courageous young warrior who sat at the controls, piloting the airboat ever further into the west. She was remembering his conduct during the terrible days and nights of their imprisonment within the bowels of the Mountains of the Terror, when death had seemed so inevitable. She herself had broken under the terror and tension of those dark hours, had been reduced to a pitiable, sobbing, helpless creature. And, now that the perils were passed and they had emerged safely from the clutches of Ningg, she recalled with a thrill of admiration the calm, unshaken courage of Diodric, his unyielding strength and fortitude, and the many small acts of courtesy, of chivalry, of thoughtfulness, he had displayed toward her when she herself had been little more than a terrified, hysteric mass of trembling fear.

In her memory she dwelt again upon his quiet, reassuring words, and upon the small and tender comforts he had given. His every thought had been to relieve her of her panic, she now realized, and she inwardly castigated herself for her inability to find the words wherewith to thank him for his kindnesses.

And there was one other thing, as well. Niane would not have been a woman had not this occurred to her also: that never once, in the many hours they had spent together in the same cell, where privacy was impossible and intimacy of a kind the young maiden had never experienced had been forced upon the two of them by their proximity and the primitiveness of their cell—never once, by word or touch or hint had he sought to take advantage of her helplessness. How many of the silken, decadent Court nobles of her acquaintance would have displayed similar restraint and chivalry under such circumstances, she wondered?

Nor would she have been fully a woman if she did not now feel a slight twinge of pique at his gentlemanly forbearance. Was it possible that—he did not find her attractive? Or was it that his heart was given to another?

Such thoughts as these, together with certain other more intimate and exciting speculations, chased themselves through the mind of the Lady Niane. Often and again her soft, dark eyes lingered on the stalwart, clean-limbed young Celt, on his yellow hair in its thick warrior's braid, on his clear, bold blue eyes under winging brows, on the square lines of his strong jaw, on his powerful and lusty young body. There were certain of these thoughts that it would have raised a blush to her cheeks to speak aloud: as it was, being even of the realm of the unspoken, they made her breath come a trifle faster and misted her great shadowy eyes.

As for Diodric, he was truly unconscious of her gaze. A change had come over the tall young Celt in the last few days. Once he had been, and had thought of himself as being, hot-blooded and impetuous and daring. The sort of fierce-hearted youth who would cut his braid and sing his Death Song in the grip of a momentary emotion. Now he was much different. Sober and thoughtful and serious—even solemn. It was responsibility that had worked this change in him. Never had Diodric been responsible for anything more than himself. But then the young and frightened girl had been thrust upon him. Suddenly he had found he could no longer afford to rush about impetuously, daring all on a risk of the dice. A new steel had entered into him.

It was partly this that had changed his manner toward Niane. He was lusty as any other young warrior—but the girl was in his charge and she was *helpless*. His sense of chivalry, his protectiveness, had changed almost into a touch of the puritanical. In the crude intimacy of the cell they had shared, the temptation to touch her, to allow a comforting, soothing hand to venture an overt caress, to permit his eyes to taste the slender softness of her body so artlessly revealed through the sorry condition of her garments, had often been well nigh irresistible. Where another man would have yielded, perhaps reluctantly, to his need—which she as well felt—he but stiffened and grew colder, wrenching his thoughts aside from this insidious channel with distaste.

But, if not conscious of her gaze, he was very conscious of her presence. She had replenished her garments from the bundle of possessions she clung to with such stubbornness, and now went robed in dark gray. But the mere closeness of her body, the physical warmth of her flesh, made his nerves tingle and his loins ache. He grimly clamped down on his jaws and drove on, forcing his thoughts to another direction.

All of these things Nephog Thoon cynically observed, his gleaming eyes laughing with mischief and mockery. It was all most amusing to the sour old fellow: but he did not laugh. Love had been denied to him by his Art: or, rather, love he had denied himseif *because* of his Art. Sensing the hunger of these healthy young bodies, the old Lemurian felt an emptiness behind his mockery. He felt somehow tired and old. Perhaps he had only now come to realize how enormous and vital and rich was the side of life he had denied himself.

They flew on.

v. Green Shadows!

It was late afternoon when the Dragon struck at last. They had flown endless leagues over the forests and plains of central Atlantis. Finally, as their hunger grew and fear of any possible pursuit faded, the Celtic warrior decided it was safe to land. They were over the jungle country now, and beyond this region lay Caiphul. But they must have food.

Diodric brought the airboat down in a shallow dive, skimming the treetops searching for a place to land. Several small streams broke the dense jungle but there was no flat, open space where he might bring them to earth in safety. At length an open glade was discerned and he dipped the prow and settled earthward.

The airboat resisted the pull of gravity and it could not be brought fully to rest upon the thick grass, but it could be moored stationary with an anchor cable. Once the ship was motionless, the Throne warrior tossed the rope ladder over the rear deck rail and helped his comrades to descend, springing lightly to the turf himself.

They were not far from a stream. While the old Lemurian sorcerer and the girl fetched clear, cold water in receptacles wherewith the craft was equipped, he went to search for meat. He had no weapon but his sword: all else, even the little holy knife that slept above his heart, had been stripped from him by the Troglodytes. He had found the sword tossed aside outside the cell when they had made their escape from the subterranean cavern world. He heartily wished he had a bow, or even the great war spear he had left behind when he deserted his post; for a sword is not a hunting weapon. You must get too close to your prey before using it. And if your prey is a deer or gazelle or even a fleet-footed goat, you have little hope of persuading the wary beast to stand still while you come near enough to kill it with your sword. However, he persevered.

And dinner literally threw itself at him.

A horrendous thundering growl shook the air. The earth erupted. Almost at his feet a great hairy boar burst into sight. Diodric caught one swift glimpse of hot, evil, little red eyes and great yellowing tusks in chomping foaming jaws before he was smashed aside by the boar's rush. A living juggernaut of meat bowled him over. Swinging its great shaggy head in a sidewise swipe, the boar sought to disembowel him in its rush—but the curved heavy tusk fouled in the tough leather of his girdle and the brute dragged the boy for some yards before realizing what had happened.

Diodric managed to keep his grip on the sword hilt; that was itself astonishing. It was even more astonishing that he lived to survive the rush of the boar; for it is one of the fiercest beasts that lived in all Atlantis, and a battling fury. Perhaps the sheer suddenness of the attack was such that he had no time to let go of the hilt. At any rate, he reached up as the boar halted its rush and stood grunting and shaking its heavy head—reached up and caught one long, hairy ear—and drove the sword deep into the thick fur of the beast's side.

The brute exploded with fury. The great head swung savagely, trying to rip his bowels out with the curved ivory knives that armed its low-slung jaws. But, although it swung Diodric half around and into the air, he retained his grip on the hilt somehow, and the strength of the beast's swing made the sword blade, buried deep in its side, tear up and into the lungs.

Crimson foam dripped from slobbering hairy lips. The boar voiced a coughing grunt. Gouts of fresh crimson stained the grass. Unsteadily, the beast sat down stumblingly. Its little red eyes were glazed. It shook its head from time to time. But it paid no more attention to the youth.

Diodric unbelted his girdle and staggered free of the injured boar. He pulled the sword out and plunged it home again, shoving it clear to the hilt. The boar coughed scarlet, shuddered, fell over, and lay still.

For dinner they had something very like roast pork. It was tough, greasy, stringy, half-raw, and half-charred from the poor fire the old sorcerer built. But the meat was hearty and they ate with vast satisfaction.

They took off before sunset. Diodric had cut

up the boar and cleaned the meat by washing it in the fresh running stream, so they carried a supply of fresh meat with them, wrapped in tough, rubbery leaves.

They were in the air only a few moments before Niane shrieked. Her slim fingers dug into Diodric's shoulder as she pointed ahead with one shaking hand.

Half a mile tall, the shadowy green figure of Thelatha straddled the horizon, searching for them.

vi. Flight Before Terror

Cold sweat stood out in great globs on the young Celt's brow and ran down his cheeks. The shadowy colossus was fantastic—beyond belief. He knew the figure at a glance. A thousand whispers told of the tall, gaunt hunched figure that went ever robed and veiled in emerald green and gloved and hooded and masked from the sight of men. He did not need the Sign of the Dragon worked on the titan's chest in black and crimson thread to know the sky-tall phantom for the Demon King.

It stood, the shadowy hem of the robes brushing the earth, lost in wooded hills, arms stretched wide as if to span from east to west, cowled head among the thin scudding clouds. It was a sight of terror beyond my words to tell. The travelers winced, sensing a cold malignant searching gaze sweep past them like the broad ray of a searchlight. It swung past once—then swung back to rivet them in the glare of unseen eyes.

One green shadowy hand—from wrist to finger-tip, it must have been more than two hundred feet long—reached for them through the thin clouds.

"By Khons, Lord of Magic!" the old Lemurian swore feebly. Then his imprecation turned into a snarling curse as he staggered and almost fell, for Diodric had swung the craft sharply to one side and sent it gliding away from the cloudy grasp of the towering phantom. The huge floating arm soared on with vast speed after them. He turned south and flew lower, his pale lips tightly pressed together, his heart thudding like a frightened bird against the cage of his ribs.

For a moment the shadowy colossus stood gazing after them. Then—suddenly—it was gone, fading from sight.

"*Ahead of us, lad!*" the old Lemurian squawked.

Directly in their path, gloom thickened, flushed with crawling emerald—and Thelatha stood with open arms as if to embrace them! Desperately, Diodric kicked the ship around and scudded off in a new direction. His blue eyes were wild with primitive terrors. Brave enough when fighting steel with steel, the primal night-fears of his savage forefathers rose within him at such a vision of horror.

Again the phantom faded from sight as they

turned away—only to reform before them, standing directly in their path. The slim *viwân* sped like a silvery arrow from side to side, but it was trapped. Nor could it rise above the colossal form of the malignant sorcerer, for the figure loomed higher than the utmost altitude the airboat could reach.

They dodged and fled and swerved and eluded —sometimes by a hair's-breadth—the clutch of the shadowy monstrous hand. It was the most harrowing battle Diodric had ever engaged in, and he saw few hopes of escaping whole from this aerial duel.

He knew the figure was no solid flesh. Some trick of the mind, some delusion of the eye, perhaps. For solid flesh it could not be. He could see through it as through a swirling dim green mist. But it was none the less terrifying for all its insubstantial aspect.

Perhaps he could fly through it unharmed. *Perhaps!* But what if he could not? What if some deadly spell struck at them while passing through the transparent shadow shape? He dared not risk the chance—oh, greatly had he changed, this boy once rash and foolhardy!

And, of course, the clutching hand caught them at last. It was bound to happen. The monstrous hand could traverse the heavens far swifter than their craft could fly the same distance. They had narrowly missed the touch of that hand a dozen times ere the end. And the end came swiftly.

The hand of Thelatha feinted—and seized at them! The light turned green and ghastly and

Diodric realized with a thrilling surge of fear they had flown *through* the green hand.

There came a bitter wintry cold, deadening, numbing. And a weird thrilling shock that blazed through every nerve-ending in their bodies. For a flashing instant, from every projection of the metal surfaces within their ship, a haze of azure flame crackled soundlessly. Diodric roared at the shock, the girl cried out. Then it was gone, leaving them numb and shaken, but—as far as they knew—unharmed.

The phenomenon was all the more terrible in that it was unknown. Much of the old science of Caiphul was forgotten in the lapse of ages. Diodric —even Nephog Thoon—had never heard of electricity. And in the ages between the fall of Lemuria and the rise of Atlantis, the knowledge of this force was lost. A Lemurian of the Elder Age could have told them that the shock of electric fire, a bolt of lightning, drains the urlium hull of an airboat of its lifting power.

They found out soon enough. Scarcely were they beyond the terrible floating hand, recovering from the ghastly thrill of terror, than the Celt saw that the *viwân* was responding sluggishly to his touch. They were losing altitude rapidly. Electric current changes the polarities of the molecular structure of urlium, the antigravity metal. But these terms would have been meaningless to our travelers.

The jungle rushed up toward them with sickening speed.

The phantom of Thelatha stood watching for a moment. Then it faded slowly from sight.

Darkness came down over the earth.

The airboat flew no longer in the skies of Atlantis.

The Demon King had created his diversion!

vii. Night-Fears

Gryphax drove his men on, hour after hour. The war birds were weary. They hungered, the great wingless birds, and their tempers grew short. Beaks clashed angrily, and they gave voice to harsh impatient cries. The cohort of Dragon warriors who rode at the heels of Gryphax were tired and hungry, too, but they knew better than to give voice to their complaints. They knew the Thurian could be merciless—coldly brutal. And they knew the thing that slept in its sheath at his side. They had seen it used. They kept their mouths closed, and rode on. Hour after hour after hour, into the thick darkness.

The three travelers made a miserable meal, hunched over a flickering fire. The wood was green and wet and smoked abominably, making their eyes smart and giving a sour taste to the boar meat. They munched their meal in silence, washing it down with clear water. All about them the mysterious jungle lay brooding and silent, veiled in night. They heard the stealthy pad of unseen feet, the rustle of gliding bodies. They felt the uncanny touch of hidden eyes.

The airboat had not crashed. Its first sickening downward rush had slackened as they grew nearer to the earth. The weird electric force that had gripped them had drained and negated most of the lifting power of the magic metal. Most; but not all. They had drifted sluggishly down, crashing through heavy branches and whipping leaves on a long slanting glide, to blunder across a clearing into a dense, thorny thicket.

They had emerged shaken, bruised, but uninjured.

But the *viwân* would fly no more.

It lay behind them now, half buried in the thicket. The shining mirror-bright metal of the trim streamlined hull was curiously dulled and lusterless, and scratched from the embrace of thorny branches.

Diodric knew the desperateness of their position. They were marooned on foot in the wilderness, still many miles from the nearest haven of refuge. They were lost in the heart of the tropic jungles that lay at the heart of western Atlantis. On foot, what speed could they make? Armed only with his blade and the unknown powers of the old Lemurian sorcerer, what chance had they to escape through the jungles unharmed and come at last to Caiphul and safety?

For that matter, which way was Caiphul—and where *were* they? In their dodging flight to elude the shadowy phantom, Diodric had lost all sense of direction. Even the old sorcerer had become confused. They discussed the problem, squatting around the smoking fire, and finally decided to wait till the light of dawn could give them some sense of east and west.

Diodric knew little of the arts of survival in the jungles of Atlantis, but he was an intelligent and resourceful youth. With his sword he cut many score of the heavy thorny branches and dragged them into a circle about the fallen craft. Surely the wicked hooked barbs would keep at bay even the hungriest and most fearless of the jungle predators. They would sleep, of course, in the fallen airboat. With dawn they must set forth on foot. Nephog Thoon believed they were somewhere in the vicinity of Naradek. Diodric had heard of this jungle river, and he had not liked the whispered tales. But the elder Lemurian claimed it led from the jungles into open country, perhaps mingling its waters with the river Nomis on whose shores rose Caiphul itself. But these problems they would leave for dawn.

They slept at last, but it was an uneasy sleep disturbed by shadowy and terrible dreams. For all the weariness of their minds and bodies, nameless night-fears haunted their slumber.

As for Nephog Thoon, the old Lemurian did not sleep. He sat wrapped in his cloak on the slanting deck, and watched the night away. He saw the far yellow spark of the planet the old Hyperborean scrolls named Cykranosh travel slowly across the dark vault of darkness and he watched the liquid brilliance of the planet Sfanomoë near the serene visage of the moon, but his thoughts were otherwhere than on astrologic configurations. Something was troubling him.

Something was also troubling the slumber of Diodric. After an uneasy sleep filled with frightful dreams of monstrous looming forms and glibbering faces, he awoke and lay on his bunk staring up into the darkness. What troubled his slumbers was an unresolved problem, an unanswered question.

Why were they so important that Thelatha employed his incredible powers to snatch them from the skies?

Toward dawn he fell into an uneasy slumber from which he was roused suddenly as the bony hand of the old Lemurian shook his naked shoulder. He started up wildly, then relaxed as he saw the drawn and worried face of the old sorcerer.

"Oh! It's you, magister. I thought—I know not what I thought," he said.

"You will be thinking many things, and soon," Nephog Thoon rasped sourly. He was distracted, and there was a shadow of unaccustomed strain and worry in his slanted eyes.

"Awaken the girl," the sorcerer said harshly. "We must be gone from this place with all speed. *Thelatha has set his warriors on our trail!* I suspected as much last night, but I was not sure. Did the Demon King force us down at random, or was there some purpose and plan in bringing us down here?"

"Well?" the boy demanded. "What think you now?"

"I do not think, I know," the Lemurian said flatly. "Last night I sent my Astral body forth into the night. There are half a thousand warriors after us, riding hard. The Demon King has given directions to find us, and commands that we be taken, and all our possessions. We must be off, and soon. Now. For they will come directly to this spot."

"I see," Diodric said thoughtfully. His brows clouded. Things were falling into place: small facts, isolated bits of puzzlement: they added up now, totaling a genuine mystery. Why had the two agents of Thelatha sought to seize the girl as she fled from the palace? Was it for herself, or for something she carried? Why had Thelatha worked mighty magic to bring them down—they were not, surely, of any importance to him? Was it something they—carried?

"What is it!" Niane called from the bunk across the cabin. Their voices, and the urgency in them, had awakened her. She half-rose, clutching her bundle to her chest, shadowy eyes enormous in her pale frightened face.

Diodric looked at her.

"My lady," he asked slowly, "what is it you guard in that bundle of clothing?"

The war birds could go no further. Gryphax

was forced to rest. His spearmen rode out as they made camp and returned, having brought down a wild aurochs of the plains. The bone-weary soldiers ate around the campfire, talking in low grunting tones almost like the grunting of animals.

Gryphax withdrew from the warriors to the deep shadows and drew forth a sphere of polished steel from his saddlebags. Into this sphere he made his report in a low voice.

"I am served by weaklings and cowards," a cold hard voice rasped in reply, sounding from empty air. The harsh, inhuman sound of that voice instinctively raised the hair on the nape of the Thurian's neck. *"However, rest if you must. But rise before dawn and press forward. They have just been awakened by the old Lemurian. He has discovered the nearness of your cohort by astral means and they will shortly leave. They will make for the River Naradek. Seek them there. They may attempt to build a raft and sail downstream for Caiphul; you must do the same."*

"I understand, Master," said Gryphax.

"See that you do more than merely understand— see that you succeed! If you fail, black dog of a Thurian, I will punish you in such a way that would strike you mad with terror if you knew of it now. Report again in seven hours!"

"Yes, Master," Gryphax said softly, but the glittering steel globe had gone dull and the heavy sense of shadowy Presence had vanished. The night air was clean and free again.

The Presence was gone, but still Gryphax sat

huddled above the sphere. Even this tenuous nearness to his dread Lord struck crawling revulsion
through his cold, grim soul. He clasped his knees
with shaking hands and his face was lowered, pale,
tense, chewing on his lips, waiting for the nausea
to recede.

Gryphax, too, had his night-fears.

viii. The Black Star Is Revealed

"My lady," Diodric said slowly, "what is it you
guard in that bundle of clothing?"

His words reverberated through the closeness of
the cabin.

"The Black Star," she said in a whisper.

"What?"

"The Black Star." The words, long pent up,
came now in a rush from her lips. She had borne
the crushing burden too long. She hungered to
share the dreadful responsibility with other,
stronger shoulders. In a tense whispering voice she
told how the Lord Guardian of the Holies had
been struck down in the very Chamber of the Hallows itself, by an agent of the Dragon—a very
brother in arms to the two masked men in black
whom Diodric had slain above her recumbent
body there on the first tier of the palace.

She could see the dawning comprehension on

the face of the young Celt. Pure, utter astonishment flooded through him. His clear blue eyes were dazed and bewildered; he stammered helpless questions.

She stopped talking and took out the Thing she had carried for so long, the precious Thing she had so carefully guarded through a thousand perils.

It was a small box of dazzling orichalc, sparkling like scarlet light. The box was no larger than a child's hand. It was superbly and beautifully made. A work of pure art, breathtaking in its complete and thrilling beauty. Slowly Diodric got off his bunk and knelt clumsily as it dawned on him what she was about to do.

Grunting and grumbling a little, favoring a certain stiffness in his joints that had come on him in the middle of his second century, the old Lemurian knelt as well.

The silence was hushed and holy.

Tenderly, she kissed the lid of the box, opened it, and drew forth That which it held.

She held it up so that they might look upon the most sacred Thing of all the earth.

The Black Star filled the darkness of the cabin with its glory.

It was not large. You could hold it in the palm of your hand like a gem. But it was rarer and more beautiful and more precious than any piece of mineral, however lovely and expensive.

The dark glory of this bit of crystal outshone all the splendor of the world.

The Gods had wrought it in the Country of the Immortals. No other Thing like this had ever been upon the earth. It was a small fragment of Paradise; it was very wonderful; the hands of the Gods had cradled it and the eyes of the Undying had peered into its bottomless depths of shimmering darkness where one elusive wisp of pure blue flame danced.

The Luck of Atlantis rested on the girl's palm. The glory of Heaven beat around her with a thousand tangling rays of shaking splendor. All hues visible to the eyes of mortal men were in that quivering aurora of supernal glory, and eleven colors otherwise not known to human vision.

While this Thing rested in the possession of the Divine Dynasty, the favor of the Gods shone upon Atlantis. No Emperor could hold the Throne unless he also held The Black Star. No usurper could seize the Throne, no invader could grasp at the pinnacle of imperial power—and hold it—without The Black Star. Oh, a city could be overthrown, a dynasty toppled, a monarch slain. But woe unto the conqueror who did not count the Luck of Atlantis among his conquests. Without this thing of crystal that was The Black Star no conqueror reigns for long.

And woe to Atlantis should it ever be lost or stolen.

Ten thousand nobly born warriors guarded it by night and day for a thousand years.

It was the Treasure of All The World.

Tears flooded the eyes of the young Celt as he knelt there on the floor of the cabin and realized the mighty honor that was his, to guard and keep safe the Holiest of All Things.

O well and wisely had old Kemthon written those words!

Never can you be certain that your life will not someday be valuable to another.

He knew that even if he were to die in the next moment of time, his name would not be forgotten on the lips of men. For all unknowingly he had guarded The Black Star, and he was *Diodric Asterion* from that first moment when he had taken the girl Niane and That which she guarded under his protection; and it was a great blessing that had come upon him, for no task among all the professions of mankind is nobler and more precious than to be a Guardian of The Black Star.

He was holy, and he knew it, and he wept like a child for he knew he was not worthy of the glory that was upon him.

They knelt there in the pallor of first dawn, the young Celtic warrior and the old Lemurian sorcerer. The heart of Diodric Asterion was filled with a blessed peace, for he had looked upon That which few among men ever dream of seeing.

Tears glistened on the wrinkled yellow cheeks of the old Lemurian thaumaturge as well, as he knelt there with bowed head in the Presence of Power. But in his heart was no blessed peace.

Bitterness and sorrow burned within him.

Alas, that it should be his cruel destiny to betray these pure and holy children who were sanctified from this moment!

But betray them he must.

Dawn flushed the skies with pale rose flame as they left the hulk of the airboat and entered the dense jungles of Atlantis. They vanished from sight in an instant, swallowed up in the green maw of the jungle.

Dawn gave them the direction. A few hours would lead them to the shores of Naradek the jungle river. From thence they could voyage downstream until Caiphul was in sight. The last stage of their journey was upon them.

But the lord Gryphax also was upon them, and half a thousand Dragon warriors thundered at his heels. He was riding fast and hard, with that grim and unswerving devotion he brought to every task set upon him by his dark Master.

They would give their lives in the defense of The Star. Of course; they knew it and welcomed the opportunity. But what if merely surrendering to death was not enough? It would be a horrible crime against the world if The Black Star were to fall into the clutches of the Dragon through their weakness or folly—or even through their strength and courage.

If Thelatha seized The Star the earth would become the domain of evil. Even the Gods could not dethrone Him Who Held The Star.

They went forward through the jungle, with all possible speed. More than this, they could not do. Perhaps it would be enough.

Perhaps.

★ 5 ★

The Book of Kashonga

The Rmoahal race came into existence
between four and five million years
ago, at which period large portions of
the great southern continent of Lemuria still existed.

It was a hot, moist country, where
huge antediluvian animals lived in
reedy swamps and dank forests.

The Rmoahals were a dark race.
Their height in these early days was
about ten or twelve feet . . . but
through the centuries their stature
gradually dwindled. They ultimately
migrated to the southern shores of
Atlantis.

—W. Scott-Elliot: *Atlantis
and the Lost Lemuria*
(edition of 1954, p. 21)

i. Green Corridors

The three travelers made their way through the dense jungles of Atlantis. Diodric led the way. The young Celt swung his steel blade, shearing through dangling vines and the thick underbrush that choked the passages between the soaring boles of mighty trees. In no time his body streamed with sweat and his bare arms and legs were scored with innumerable scratches from the thorned lianas and the whipping of sharp-edged leaves. He ignored these discomforts, and made what progress he could.

At times, even his sword was inadequate to the task of clearing a path through the crowded green corridors of the jungle. Then the old Lemurian sorcerer was forced to employ the dwindling energies of his wizard's Staff. He would step forward and thrust the black rod toward the thicket.

Fierce brilliance would flare into momentary being. Shriveling, blackening, the vegetation would wither aside from the searing flash of intolerable light.

They continued. The unfortunate thing about all of this was that in clearing their path they left an unmistakable trail for the Dragon cohort to follow. And Nephog Thoon assured them that Gryphax and his warriors were moving forward with all possible speed, hoping to cut them off before they reached the shores of the jungle river. During infrequent rest stops, the old Lemurian would employ his Astral vision to ascertain the ever-shrinking interval between the pursuers and the pursued.

Several factors weighed heavily on their side. For one thing, they were some hours ahead of the servants of the Demon King. For another, it was easier for three persons to force passage through the green aisles of the jungle than for half a thousand men and war birds. They could move faster and slip through slender interstices in the dense emerald growth; but the Dragon warriors must pause many times to hack a wider way for their passage.

Niane almost forgot her fears amidst the beauty of their surroundings. The jungle is a terrifying place by night, when unseen slinking things creep flame-eyed through dense darkness and the gloom is made hideous with the thunderous growls of the mighty predators and the agonized screams of their prey. But by day the jungle is a fairyland of incredible beauty. Lofty boles soar like the columns of a great cathedral. Through the mosaic of whispering leaves and arched branches that form the jungle's roof, slanting beams of sungold filter down to splash the grassy turf with wavering puddles of liquid fire. All else is drowned in a mystic emerald twilight, filled with whispers and the far, weird cry of exotic jungle birds.

Here and there amazing flowers bloom among thick glossy leaves. Blossoms of enormous size and startling beauty in a bewildering variety of shades and colors. Their heady perfumes, mingling with the odorous gums of tropic trees, added to the templelike atmosphere of the scene.

They moved on through the hushed solemnity of the green twilight.

The heavy silence of the dim jungle grew oppressive. More to break the hushed stillness than for any other reason, the travelers began discussing the story of The Black Star, which tailsman now rested in its glittering casket of orichalc over Diodric's heart, securely nested in the breast of his leathern tunic.

"It is a great puzzle to me that the Divine One could have fled from the palace, leaving The Star behind," the young warrior confessed as they slogged along through heavy bushes.

"I have wondered about that myself," the girl admitted. "I can only assume that the decision to abandon the City came at the last possible moment, and in the rush and confusion of the unexpected departure of the Court, no one observed that certain members of the Imperial party were still absent in far portions of the palace. Surely, others besides myself failed to rejoin the Emperor's group when it fled the City."

Nephog Thoon cleared his throat. "The Lord Guardian of the Holies, this Rhamsheth Asterion of whom you spoke, he must have gone directly to the Chamber to secure The Star, as was his responsibility. But he encountered one of the masked assassins of Thelatha in the very act of theft, slew him and was injured, and could not rejoin the Divine Pnomphis in time."

The girl nodded wearily. "That must have been how it happened," she said. "With so many courtiers milling about, the Emperor must have assumed that Lord Rhamsheth was among them, and thus gave the signal to depart. Everything was in such a whirling chaos of confusion during those last stages before the escape of the Imperial party, that it is easy enough to understand how the Emperor could take it for granted the Lord Guardian had returned."

"I suppose you are right, my lady," Diodric mused. "No one would have any reason to guess that anything could delay Lord Rhamsheth. It was a logical assumption to make—but a tragic error, nonetheless."

To this summing-up the others could only agree.

"I wonder what will happen if the Dragon does not secure The Star," the youth mused. The old Lemurian sorcerer grunted sourly.

"Who can say?" he rasped. "But I can tell you this: he will not for long hold empery over the Throne of Atlantis. The Gods will strike him down in flame and thunder, or so the old scrolls predict. But neither can the White Emperor retain his claim to the Throne of Atlantis without that he hath possession of the Great Talisman. It hath been the decree of Heaven from the birth of the Second Empire that no man may hold the kingship of Atlantis without The Black Star."

Diodric chewed over this thought in silence for a moment. They had just entered a small, open glade and had reached its heart. He opened his mouth to make some comment in reply to the words of the old Lemurian.

But the words were never given utterance— for then a striped horror struck like a thunderbolt!

ii. Fang-Mouth

Thick, glossy leaves exploded into motion. From the dense thicket directly in their path, across a small glade or clearing, erupted a fantastic monster. Like a living thunderbolt of tawny flesh it crashed amongst them, sending the three adventurers reeling to either side. One enormous paw flashed out and struck the Staff from the hands of the old sorcerer. The mighty wand of power was tossed into the underbrush and Nephog Thoon staggered back with a cry, searching his mind for a potent rune whose utterance might strike down the snarling colossus.

Diodric sprang to his feet in a lithe bound, whipping his sword about, shouting hoarse commands for the others to take cover in the heavy underbrush. The old Lemurian plunged into the dark bushes to recover his Staff. Niane had shrieked and fled into the gloom on the other side of the glade. The Throne warrior faced the snarling horror alone.

He had never seen such a monster before. It was a great tawny cat, thirteen feet long from snarling muzzle to the tip of its lashing tail. Its lean silken-furred sides were marked with jagged black lines. A rumble of blood-freezing menace sounded from its mighty chest, as the terror-cat crouched against the floor of the clearing, its burning gaze fixed on the desperate face of the young warrior.

Never had Diodric seen such a beast, but he had heard travelers whisper of such a monster. *Fang-Mouth,* the Rmoahal savages who dwelt in these jungles, called it: the name is as good as any. For from the snarling black jaws of the ferocious head extended two terrible scimitars of glistening ivory. The very length of those curved and sword-like fangs would strike terror into the heart of the bravest of warriors. Usually, Fang-Mouth dwelt in the caves of the rocky hill country; but betimes, when game was scarce, a few of the cats would be driven by the pangs of hunger to venture down into the jungles of Atlantis. Such was the case at present. Intolerable hunger blazed in the burning eyes that fixed Diodric in their glare. Foaming saliva drooled from the yawning jaws of the brute. Diodric could see the ribs along the heaving sides of the striped body. Terrific hunger had goaded the devil-cat into a murderous fury. At any moment the creature would attack. And the young warrior had naught but the sword wherewith to combat that snarling engine of destruction. The sword in his hands was useless. It could inflict little more than a pin prick, which would only further enrage the half-maddened beast, whose tawny, rippling body was the length of two full-grown men.

Helpless, feeling the icy breath of Doom against his naked flesh, the young Celt crouched with his sword clenched in one strong hand—awaiting the murderous charge of the terrible sabre-toothed tiger, one of the most ferocious man-killers of the ancient primitive world.

iii. The Blue Man

Niane fled down the jungle path on frantic, stumbling feet. Her gown was torn. Her slim white legs were scratched and bleeding. She panted for breath, young breasts heaving and straining against the fabric of her gown. She had no doubt that the fantastic devil-cat had slaughtered both of her comrades, and she dreaded, with each passing moment, to hear the stealthy slither of its tawny, jagged-marked hide as it came padding down the aisle to sate its blood lust on her tender flesh.

She had no idea in which direction her panic-stricken flight had taken her. A thick canopy of leaves arched like a domed roof far above her head, cutting away the sight of the sky. Helpless to ascertain the position of the sun, she could have no knowledge where she was going. Many times she tripped in tangling vines and fell to lie cushioned in fallen leaves or thick grasses, sobbing with exhaustion and terror. The futility of flight gradually dawned upon her. The tawny horror could slink through the jungle aisles at many times the speed at which she could flog her exhausted body to attain.

And, what was far worse than her own demise under the terrible slashing fangs—*The Black Star was lost!*

Doubtless it lay still hidden over the dead heart of the youth, Diodric. A pang of loss went through her as she thought of that strong young body now torn and crimsoned and forever still. His death had come to him through her. The dawning love which had begun to blossom within her added to the poignant pain a sense of greater loss.

With all at an end—what use for her to cling to life?

The weary girl dragged herself to her feet again and turned, and went back along the way that she had come.

If death must come to her here in the green heart of the trackless jungles, she could think of no more fitting agent for her destruction than the tearing fangs of the great cat that had crushed out the life of the young warrior she now realized she loved.

Back toward the clearing she bent her way. She dreaded the scene of scarlet horror she would find at the end of the trail. But she went forward with serenity in her heart.

When all is lost, no further loss has power to hurt.

It was perhaps an hour later. Niane sank wearily to her knees and put her face in her hands. She knew now that she was hopelessly lost in the dim and tangled ways of the impenetrable jungle. She had thought to retrace her steps, but this had at length proven more difficult than ever she had dreamed. For in the twilit gloom, every path looks very much like every other. And so overwhelming had been the terror of her flight that she had not paused to observe any landmarks. By now, she was completely confused and her innate sense of direction was totally helpless to assist.

As she knelt there, exhausted, sobbing, she heard a sudden sound in the underbrush to her left.

A sharp thrill of fear ran through her. Scarce daring to breathe, the girl lifted her face from her hands and searched the dense wall of foliage with wide eyes. The sound had resembled the snapping of a dry twig. *Had* some slinking predator crept upon her as she knelt sobbing, abandoning all caution to the tempest of her emotions?

She searched the surrounding floor of the jungle for some weapon with which to defend herself. Alas, there was nothing to hand but dead rotting leaves and wet grasses. Not even a rock, a bit of wood, could she see.

Her only hope lay in flight.

Gone now were her morbid thoughts of self-extinction—of hurling her frail body into the crushing jaws of the striped and tawny devil-cat whom she believed had slain her lover and the old Lemurian. Young vigorous life sought only to live another hour—another minute—another heartbeat.

She turned to flee swift-footed down the path by which she had come. But in the next instant it was too late. A gigantic form stepped from the wall of leaves to face her with cold impassive eyes!

A shape of terror—a naked giant of a man, bald and blue-black of skin—nine feet tall the silent savage stood, and one mighty hand clenched a great bow whose stone-tipped arrow was nocked and drawn and pointing directly at her heart!

iv. The Horror in the Pit

It would not have been in the character of the bold young Celtic warrior to have stood idly and helplessly, waiting the killing charge of the snarling sabre-toothed tiger.

Diodric whirled and sprang from the clearing, vanishing into the thick wall of leaves that bordered one side of the small glade.

He found himself in shadowy twilight, broken only by dim shafts of radiance where the bright sphere of Polinax far above broke through the canopy of leaves overhead, to dance in trembling blobs of light against the boles of mighty trees. A clear avenue lay ahead of him and without pausing for a moment the Celt raced from the scene.

It was not cowardice that forced him to flee—but courage. He could not defend his companions by standing there, waiting to be struck down by that snarling juggernaut of tawny murder. By his flight he could perchance draw the devil-cat further away from the direction in which the girl and the old Lemurian had doubtless fled. He drove strength into his racing feet in desperate flight. Every second he could elude Fang-Mouth gave him a further margin of safety, a greater chance at surviving.

A thunderous howl of frustrated fury and blood-lust exploded from the glade behind him. In a single great bound, the monstrous cat tore through the bushes after him, gaining on him with incredible speed. Glancing back over his shoulder, Diodric saw the cat was only a dozen paces behind him. He turned on impulse and went crashing through the thickets that lined the jungle aisle.

Leaves whipped his face, lashed his bare arms, blinded his eyes. A thousand twigs, like bony fingers, plucked and snagged and tore at the rags of his leathern tunic. Ignoring the torment of the goring twigs and slashing leaves, he plunged ever deeper into the dense underbrush.

He could hear no sound behind him. Had the monstrous cat lost his trail—was it possible? Or did the wary brute, for some unknown reason, choose to turn aside and seek a less elusive prey? Another thought came to the panting young warrior as he forced a passage through the crackling branches: perhaps the jungle terror knew a swifter route! Perhaps, when he burst at last through the thicket, he would find the great cat waiting for him, crouched with glaring eyes and twitching tail for the murderous rush of the charge.

He pressed on, and suddenly tore through the heavy thicket to find himself on the edge of yet another glade. Dim gloom obscured his sight, but he could see that this secluded clearing was larger than the one in which the beast had first attacked them. It was paved with layer after layer of rotting leaves. He sprinted across it, knowing that safety lay in the thick-packed jungle, not in such an open space—

Halfway across the clearing the earth suddenly gave way beneath his feet and he fell.

A cry of despair was torn from his lips as the blackness swallowed him. Twisting like a cat, he snatched frantically at the edge of the pit. His fingers closed over a branch—slipped on the wet bark—then clung.

He dangled in the gloom of the pit. The branch creaked ominously under his weight. At any instant it might give way and precipitate him into the unknown depths of darkness below.

He shifted his weight, striving to reach a higher branch. He could see now that this was a pit trap, such as the savage Rmoahal tribesmen dig for unwary beasts. A great hole is dug in the earth and covered with branches which are then strewn with leaves. The bottoms of such pits are usually set with shafts of wood sharpened at one end, the blunt end buried in the earth so that they point upward to impale the falling beasts who stumble into the trap.

Had it not been for his luck in catching one of the roof branches, he might now hang impaled on the sharpened shafts below.

The branch cracked with a deafening sound, and he fell. But in falling he twisted his body to one side and crashed down in a corner of the pit, landing in soft earth, managing to avoid the sharpened stakes. As it was, the breath was knocked from his body by the impact and he lay gasping for air for some time. Then, rising to his feet the young warrior began to prowl the depths of the pit trap. He soon realized he was hopelessly imprisoned. The mouth of the pit was twenty feet above his head, and the walls were sheer, of hard-packed earth which nonetheless would crumble under his weight. He tried to climb them thrice, digging foot- and hand-holds with the point of his sword, and proved this last point beyond question.

But the full horror of his situation had yet to dawn on him.

It was not until he heard a soft deep-throated growl and looked up to stare directly into the foaming jaws and burning gaze of the giant tiger where it crouched with lashing tail at the mouth of the pit that he came to realize just how hopelessly he *was* trapped!

v. The Magic of Nephog Thoon

When the flashing paw of the giant saber-tooth struck the Staff spinning from his grip into the underbrush, Nephog Thoon felt a moment of depthless horror. The stave of a wizard is to him a tool, a weapon, an instrument, and the insignia and scepter of his power. Unarmed, the old Lemurian sorcerer felt divested of his magistery.

Thus, he shrank from the snarling maw of the jungle horror, and took to his heels, plunging into the wall of rustling leaves. If he could regain his Staff of Power, the old sorcerer knew, he could hold off a hundred such devil-cats. Without the Staff, he felt helpless.

He continued forward for some time through the dense thicket and emerged at length into one of the maze of green corridors that laced the jungle. He had not the slightest idea of the direction in which he had come, and such had been the extremity of his terror, that he had only the vaguest notion of how long he had been struggling through the underbrush.

He only knew that he had not found his Staff.

The Lemurian sorcerer turned his gaze on the thicket from which he had come. His only hope lay in re-entering it and thus hoping to locate the lost Staff. But every fiber of the old man's being revolted at the notion of retracing his steps, perhaps to find himself facing that snarling jungle killer at the end of his path once again. Yet without his Staff he was as helpless as would be any other frail, elderly gentleman of two hundred and nine years of age. It was an insoluble dilemma, and he pondered it for some moments while regaining his breath and quieting his racing heartbeat.

The Staff of a magician is keyed to the vibrations of his personal aura, attuned to the frequency of his mind, in resonance with his own life force. There exists a tenuous, but nonetheless substantial, bond between the Staff and him who wields it. Nephog Thoon believed he could bend that tenuous linkage to his own uses.

He focused his mind on the Staff, picturing it in every detail, its length and weight, the very feel of it in his palm, the sheen of the ancient ebony, the minute gold hieroglyphics that coiled in a spiral about the length.

Holding this picture in his mind with considerable effort, the old Lemurian summoned the dormant powers within his being, and uttered a Spell of Force. The strange syllables reverberated in the hushed jungle still. Each phonemic grouping set up its own web of crosscurrents which subtly blended and subtly contrasted with the phonemes already set into aural motion. The fabric of space/time shivered, and displaced itself in a very small way. At the feet of the wizard, a broken branch snapped out of existence.

And the Staff flashed into being and lay quivering at his feet.

Grinning, the old sorcerer bent over and picked it up and hefted it with satisfaction. He beamed on the jungle, with a rare smile. Let come what may: with the Staff of Power in his hand, he felt ready for anything!

All afternoon Nephog Thoon wound his way through the jungle maze, getting hotter and wearier and angrier with every hour that passed. He knew very well in which direction his friends were, for he could perceive this on the Astral plane. But it seemed impossible for him to find his way to them. The winding jungle ways, the lack of a clear sight of the sun, the confusion of trees and bushes that looked exactly like a thousand other trees and bushes he had passed this day, all conspired to twist utterly awry his sense of direction.

At length he sat down grumpily on a fallen log and conjured into being a drink of cold wine. It took a considerable degree of Power, and normally he would have gone thirsty rather than so deplete his ever-dwindling reserves of magical energy, but he heartily damned all prudence and caution. He was thirsty and he would drink. A chilled flagon of a tangy beverage brewed in the hills of southern Adalon snapped into existence with a twang of displaced air. He emptied the pitcher with gusto, smacking his lips with pleasure.

And then he heard the outriders.

His nape prickled. The sounds of many men moving through the jungle became audible. Many men and war birds, moving this way. He sprang to his feet in alarm: surely it could be none other than the cohort of Dragon warriors who had tirelessly followed their trail from the City of the Golden Gates. The old Lemurian went cold at the thought. Again he employed his Astral senses to ascertain the position and number of the foe, and his skin crawled with horror as he realized the forces of Lord Gryphax had lost the trail of the fugitives and had thus spread out into a broad crescentiform front and were literally combing the jungle.

And he was directly in their path!

vi. The Robe of Confusion

The discovery unmanned the old Lemurian sorcerer. For a long moment he just stood there, feebly cursing with an extensive vocabulary in twelve languages, three of which were not spoken upon the earth and two of which were never intended to be spoken aloud by beings of flesh. He cursed his dull wits, wondering what to do.

How could he hide from them? His old bones were too weary to attempt anything as physical as climbing a tree—even if any of the trees about had branches low enough to make the attempt possible. But they were komis trees, from the dark scarlet of their bark, and their branches grew twenty or thirty feet up the tall smooth boles. He might be able to conceal himself from view by huddling in the middle of a bush, but what if he were discovered? He could just imagine the loud guffaws, the rude remarks, the miserable spectacle he would make if discovered and dragged from the bush—the great Lemurian magister, huddled beneath a bush, curled up like a great ungainly animal! He would rather die where he stood than hide in such a manner, with the risk of discovery hanging over his head.

Hide.

He closed his eyes and smacked his brow sharply with the palm of one bony hand. By Khons the Lord of Magic, his mind was wandering—he was losing his wits, and here he was hardly into his third century! How could he have forgotten the other major implement of magic he had fetched all the way from his tower in the foothills of the Mountains of the Terror? Had he borne the knapsack strapped to his gaunt shoulders for so long that he had forgotten what it held? Hastily, with shaking fingers, grumbling curses and imprecations under his breath, the old sorcerer wriggled out of the straps and opened the sack, drawing forth a most peculiar garment.

It was called, in the manuals of sorcery, a Robe of Confusion. But it was more of a cloak than a robe, and fashioned from a stiff glassy fabric, on the one side, and a deep, soft, midnight-black cloth on the outer side. The robe had two purposes, but Nephog Thoon had the second of these in mind. Hence he swiftly turned the robe inside out so that the glassy, crackling surface met the eye. Hastily, he donned the Robe of Confusion, drawing the voluminous sleeves down so that they covered his hands, adjusting the long hem so that it concealed his buskins, and pulling the heavy cowl up around his face. He was thus completely hidden in the folds of the glistening, peculiar fabric, which was not cloth but akin to woven metal or rather a tissue of metal, created by fire magic.

The glassy metallic tissue had an odd quality. The eye slid off it in a strange manner: the gaze was baffled and turned aside. The strange, eye-wrenching and glistening tissue was oddly difficult to see. In a word, it *resisted* being seen, as a wax-impregnated cloth resists wetting.

Thus hidden in the Robe of Confusion, Nephog Thoon stood motionless in the shadows of a stand of tall trees and waited. The first scouts of the pursuit party came into view. They were tattered, bedraggled, hot, tired, and short of temper. Gryphax obviously had driven them hard all day.

Through mica-shielded eye-holes in the cowl of the cloak, Nephog Thoon eyed the warriors of Thelatha with intense curiosity. He had heard much of the Chaos-worshipers, but had never seen them so close before. He remembered that the cult of black magicians, whose head the Demon King had become, had been outlawed and driven into exile from Atlantis seventeen years earlier. The Dragon had fled into the southern tropics of the continent of Thuria to the east of Atlantis across the Gorgonian Sea. There, in the black jungles of Tartarus, he had recruited the first of his horde from among the savage warriors of the Dark Kingdom. From the fiendish barbarians of the land of Gorgonia had come primal Shemitish devil worshipers to swell his growing horde, and from among the shadow-haunted tombs of southern Khem-

Mu had he found yet more to follow the banners of Chaos.

Nephog Thoon thus saw the rumors were true, for many of the cohort now passing through his region of the jungle were the swarthy nomads of Khem-Mu, the black savages of jungled Tartarus who were reputedly degenerate descendants of the once mighty Rmoahal race, largely driven from Atlantis ages ago, and the strange, squat, hairy, cold-eyed little fiends of Gorgonia, who worshiped a nameless goddess whose blasphemous idols depicted a smiling and beautiful woman with a writhing crown of snakes for hair. Among such degenerate scum the Dragon had found the nucleus of his army, wherewith he had returned in strength across the Gorgonian Sea to invade the shores of the Sacred Island of Atlantis.

The warriors were all around him now. The old sorcerer wondered which one was Gryphax. He saw many of the Priests of Chaos among the troop. It was known that the gaunt, skull-faced, black-robed shamans with the Ouroboros symbol on the chest of their robes went always among the warriors to search out the least signs of weakness, or heresy, or of the softer emotions—which were ruthlessly expunged in blood.

One of these tall robed men with a shaven pate and keen quick eyes rode past the place where Nephog Thoon was standing. The war bird shied, sensing the presence of the invisible sorcerer, squawking in dismay. And Nephog Thoon felt his liver go cold at the chance of discovery.

The Priest of Chaos halted the bird, and turned to search the shadows with sharp-eyed scrutiny. Nephog Thoon sucked in his breath, not daring to move a muscle. The Robe of Confusion would wrench and bend awry the gaze of a mortal eye on the Physical plane . . . he only hoped the vile Chaos-worshiper would not employ a higher level of vision. For the glassy metallic tissue was not proof to the eye of Astral sight.

Alas, his fears were not groundless. The priest closed the eyes of his physical body. On the Astral level, he opened the Ajnaic Chakra that was the Astral eye—and saw the Lemurian!

He opened his mouth to cry an alarm.

Well, sighed the old sorcerer, the game was up. He swung up his Staff and blew the Priest of Chaos out of the saddle with a shaft of blazing lightning.

In a thrice, hundreds of warriors were milling about, swords out and war horns sounding the alarm. Nephog Thoon ground out a bitter curse and metaphorically rolled up his sleeves and began to fight for his life. The Staff contained many lightnings, but not enough to account for half a thousand well-armed Dragon warriors. Well, he could not help that.

He would take as many as he could with him, he determined, before he went down into the Kingdom of Darkness.

Invisible, his Staff spitting bolts of lightning fire, the old sorcerer began his mightiest battle.

It was soon over.

vii. The Battle in the Pit

Fang-Mouth was uneasy. He could smell the hot stench of living man-flesh in the dark pit beneath his paws, but he did not like the idea of going down into that black hole in the earth. He prowled back and forth along the margin of the pit, pausing from time to time to give voice to an earth-shaking bellow of rage.

From time to time he paused and hovered on the margin of the pit trap. His blazing eyes could discern the sharpened stakes, but the fierce, cunning mind behind those eyes did not understand them. The mighty saber-tooth was cunning enough to detect their menace, but hunger so clouded his small, dark brain that his wary intelligence was distracted. For seven days the great cat had taken no meat. Hunger was a raging, furious demon pent up in his hollow belly. It slashed with razoring claws, demanding food. Fang-Mouth eyed the sharpened stakes suspiciously. His distended nostrils could smell them from here. They stank of death; they reeked of fear. But the clamoring fiend in his belly drowned out the faint sense of warning.

The man-thing moved below. It was desperately tugging one of the sharp stakes up from the

earth. It hefted the long shaft—weighed it like a
spear. Fang-Mouth had seen spears before in the
hands of a man-thing. He knew they caused hurt.
Along the sliding thews of his mighty shoulder ran
a long, jagged, glassy scar from just such a pointed
throwing-stick, taken a year before in battle with
a blue savage.

But all this clamored in vain for attention.
Fang-Mouth paid no attention to the warnings.
His mind was crowded with tantalizing images:
the crunch of his powerful jaws tearing and ripping through flesh; the screaming, kicking thing
struggling against the closing vise of those great
and terribly-armed jaws; the spurt of hot gore;
the snap and crunch of bones crushed in his massive jaws; the long, gorging feast that would follow; the delicious feeling of repletion when, his
growling belly filled with succulent man-flesh, the
mighty jungle killer would creep sluggishly away
to its lair, there to slumber through the daylight
hours. Such images filled his small, fierce brain,
and almost made him mad with the lust to kill.

At last, Fang-Mouth could endure the waiting
no longer. Crouching on the edge of the pit, motionless save for the quivering of his haunches and
the lashing of his tail, he gathered himself for the
great leap. The long tail ceased movement
abruptly—a ripple of tension ran through the body
that was now motionless as a graven image.

And he sprang.

Sweat gathered on Diodric's brow and ran

down his face, blurring his vision. His torso glistened wetly. But he stood, watching the prowling saber-tooth, hands clenched about the shaft of the sharpened stake. It was the best weapon he could find, but he doubted that it would be effective against so awesome an engine of destruction as the giant cat. If he could be certain of driving the shaft directly through that savage heart—yes. But a hair's-breadth error to one side or another, and—

Just then it paused motionless, and his heart stopped. He took his stand, spreading his legs and bending his knees slightly, so as to absorb the impact of the cat's spring. The stake he held slanting upward.

It sprang like a flash of tawny lightning.

At the last half-second before it leaped, a sudden uproar of shouting, screaming men sounded in the distance, together with a series of inexplicable thunder-crashes. The cat had already begun its leap when the sudden clamor unnerved it, and it leaped slightly off-balance. Squalling and spitting with fury, the tawny-furred thunderbolt crashed down on Diodric.

Desperately, he shifted his stance to account for the altered direction—but it was too late. The stake tore into the great, gliding thews of the shoulder, but came nowhere near a vital organ.

The hot slash of pain along its shoulder goaded the brute into an explosion of fury. It whipped about, striking from side to side with slashing paws. Each paw weighed thirty pounds, and the blows were like sledge hammers. It had landed on the soft earth beyond the up-thrusting forest of stakes. Now, its dim, maddened brain equating the silent standing sticks with the lash of white-hot pain it had received from the stick in the hands of the man-thing, it turned the hammering fury of those massive paws on the stakes. Whole rows of them were torn out of the earth, or shattered aside. Squalling with incandescent fury, the injured cat rampaged among the stakes while Diodric, still clutching his rude spear, backed across the pit. He had seconds to live, and he knew it.

A sudden idea came to him. He drew up the stake like a javelin and hurled it straight at the cat, whose back was to him as it roared and raged among the forest of stakes. The cast took the brute squarely between the shoulders, but either Diodric had miscalculated the strength required to cast the spear so far, or it was heavier than he had realized—for the pointed tip only penetrated a few inches into the sliding sheaths of tough muscle. Far from taking a deadly wound, the injury inflicted by the thrown stake only reminded the tormented and furious cat of its man-prey.

It whirled to face him, long streamers of foaming slaver whipping from its black, wet, snarling jaws. The ivory sabers glistened wetly. The red eyes burned like coals of furious hate. It came at him with a breathtaking rush—and stopped as suddenly as if it had run into a wall!

Diodric blinked; gasped; looked again.

A gigantic spear, flashing from nowhere in an

instant, pinned the squalling cat to the earth!

The spear was twelve feet long and bladed with keen steel. It had been thrown with terrific force, for the blow had driven the spearhead through one shoulder, down through the entire breadth of the mighty chest, and deep into the earth below, thus riveting the tiger to the earth as an insect is transfixed with a long pin.

Blood gushed from the jaws of the tiger as its fangs clashed and gnawed in a fury of agony, crunching through and through the shaft of the spear. Blood gouted from the open jaws. The beast coughed hollowly and sagged, head wavering. The burning eyes glazed and went cold. The great head drooped as if exhausted. The cat was dead.

Diodric could hardly believe his eyes. He staggered over to peer at the enormous javelin. He recognized the markings, the tuft of bird-feathers near the hilt, the parallel slashes of blue pigment near the head. *A Rmoahal war spear!*

A snapping twig above him jerked him half around. He stared up into the cold, impassive gaze of the mighty, blue-black, half-naked Rmoahal savage who stood above him, a second spear poised for the hurling.

viii. Kashonga

It was a dazed, confused young Celt who came clambering up out of the pit, clinging to the severed length of liana the giant, blue-skinned savage had let down to him. And hardly had he come sprawling up over the edge to stand, however shakily, on the surface of the earth again, when Niane threw herself upon him with inarticulate cries of joy. She wrapped her bare arms about his neck and lifted her tear-stained, begrimed face to him to be kissed.

He was not too confused to realize when a girl wants to be kissed. So—with the half-naked giant standing by, observing these goings-on with an impassive dignity, arms folded upon his mighty breast —Diodric kissed the girl. And that, soundly.

There was hardly time for introductions, much less for explanations. The air was full of smoke and the screams of frightened men and men in pain drifted to them. Half the jungle was ablaze and the Rmoahal—his name, it seemed, was Kashonga— could lead them to the river that was the only place of safety with fire loose among the thick-set trees. Diodric had heard of the uncanny sense of direction which was Nature's gift to her gigantic, blue-skinned children, so he permitted the burly savage to take the lead without a quibble. Kashonga immediately headed off at a rapid pace without a moment's hesitation, the two young people at his heels.

As they made their way through the smoke-filled aisles of the jungle, Niane gasped out an abbreviated account of what had happened. She had become lost after they parted in the clearing, and the Rmoahal giant had found her. He was aware that a cohort of Dragon warriors had entered the jungle in pursuit of them—"the Witchmen" he called them, grunting with contempt. Any foe of the Witchmen was a friend of the towering blue giant, for the servants of Thelatha had come through these jungles half a year ago, slaughtering all his tribe, using the women for their pleasure before cutting their throats, bearing off the children for slaves, and disposing of the wounded, the sick, and the elderly by the simple expediency of leaving them bound and helpless in their reed huts—which they then set afire. Of all his people, Kashonga alone had lived, and he had sworn before the rude altars of his savage gods unsleeping vigilance and hatred against all Witchmen.

Thus the mighty Rmoahal had assisted the girl to rejoin her comrades. He had swiftly and unerringly tracked the path of Diodric's flight, coming to the mouth of the pit trap just in time to strike down the squalling saber-tooth with one of the two great war spears he carried.

As they hurried through the burning jungle, Diodric exchanged a few words with the impassive Rmoahal. No, he did not know what had set the jungle afire. Nor did he know the whereabouts of the third of their company—he had not seen Nephog Thoon. Doubtless the old man had perished either at the hands of the Dragon warriors, or in the raging inferno that thundered behind them at their heels.

They went crashing through the underbrush, Kashonga clearing a path by swinging his great spear to left and right as if it were a two-handed broadsword. Curiously, they encountered not a single Dragon warrior in their flight. Kashonga grunted a curt explanation for this. The wall of fire had sprung into being between them and the curved front of the Chaos warriors, thus cutting their pursuers off.

"You have certainly saved my life, and the life of the Lady Niane as well, Kashonga," Diodric said warmly. "We cannot thank you enough for your assistance."

The towering giant nodded with majestic dignity. "You fight Witchmen," he grunted. "That is good! I fight Witchmen too—" he touched a row of small withered things which dangled at his waist, bound to his girdle with leathern thongs. They looked like dry twigs. Glancing closer, Diodric realized with a little thrill of horror that each of the objects was *a human forefinger!*

"I, too, kill many Witchmen," Kashonga said simply.

There were nineteen of the withered fingers dangling from his girdle like a grisly fringe.

It was late afternoon before they reached the river. They had gone stumbling along in the wake of the striding giant for hours without pause for rest. Then, and suddenly, they burst from the edge of the jungle into matted reeds and muddy shallows. Swift-flowing water stretched as far as the eye could see in either direction. The river was some two hundred yards wide at this point. It was good to look on the dark, rushing water mirroring the late afternoon sky above, reflecting the crimson conflagration of the sunset in the west. So they had reached Naradek at last! The road to Caiphul lay open before them.

But there was yet another surprise in store.

They moved along the edge of the river, searching for fallen logs wherewith to build a raft. The wall of flames was advancing toward them step by blazing step. They would only be safe in the midst of moving waters. But the sword of the Celtic warrior could hardly cut through a dozen tree trunks in time. They must find and lash together fallen logs, and launch themselves upon the river without delay.

Suddenly Diodric, who was leading the way, stopped short so suddenly that Niane jostled into him and almost pitched him headfirst into the mud. The Celt stared—and burst into hearty laughter.

"I guess nothing can kill a Lemurian!" he laughed.

Niane blinked incredulous eyes. There, seated atop a neat stack of some seventeen logs, Nephog Thoon sat smirking at them with satisfaction.

"How . . . ? Where . . . ?" the girl spluttered.

The old sorcerer smirked, adjusting his skullcap neatly.

"I—ah—thought you might be able to use these," he said, gesturing in an off-handed manner to the pile of logs. "A little magic comes in handy," he added modestly.

Diodric shrugged wordlessly. "And I suppose you are also responsible for all *that?*" he remarked, gesturing at the distant glow of the fire. The old Lemurian shrugged and permitted himself another few chuckles.

"I, too, can create a little—diversion," he said, smugly.

Kashonga stood, listening to this interchange with an expression of unruffled dignity that concealed an almost total lack of comprehension. These small pale people spoke a strange language among themselves, he doubted if he would ever come to understand them.

However, they killed Witchmen. That was all he needed to know about the small ones. They were friends.

He set about building a raft to carry them to Caiphul.

ix. The Battle on Naradek River

Gryphax stood watching his men laboring beside the river. Night had long since fallen. The stars blazed far above, but the moon was hidden behind roiling clouds of black smoke. The Dragon captain was bone-weary, his face a black mask of soot, his left hand bandaged and numbed. The raging fire had taken a heavy toll of his troops: ninety-three of his cohort had died in the mysterious blaze. And there was no accounting for the mysterious disaster. It was as if some invisible thing had walked among them, hurling thunderbolts to left and right. Several of the Priests of Chaos had died by the sizzling bolts. Whole squadrons of Dragon warriors, unfortunately clustered together, had perished from the mysterious attack. Then the rain of levin-bolts had set the jungle underbrush afire. For hours his men had battled the blaze that stood between them and their prey like a wall of woven flames. Dozens of his warriors had been burned alive, caught in the flaming underbrush or pinned beneath fallen trees that blazed like oil-soaked torches. Others had perished by the score from smoke inhalation. At length they had fought their way to the edge of the river, only to find their prey long since departed and doubtless far downstream by now.

In the pitch-black night, the remainder of the cohort labored to build gigantic rafts. Gryphax tightened his lips grimly, his gaunt face strained and ghastly with tension. He would keep them at this task all night long without rest, if need be. They *must* catch up with the guardians of The Black Star. And they would. Soon. *Soon!*

For two days the travelers poled downriver. Walls of green foliage slid past on either side and the blue sky arched above. Kashonga and Diodric took turns at the poles, but the current was so swift that little work was required save for steering. The weird cry of jungle birds came to them over the rushing waters, and the coughing grunt of prowling beasts. Of their pursuers, they saw no sign although the dour old sorcerer assured them Gryphax still followed.

Standing at the pole, swaying with the movements of the raft, feeling the warm sun on his thighs and arms and the wind riffling his thick, yellow hair, a vast peace filled the young Celt. There had been no time for words between Niane and himself, and no privacy, but an unspoken rapport had been established and from time to time they looked deeply into each other's eyes or exchanged a slow smile. In these interchanges, there was a depth of meaning that went beyond mere words. Diodric was filled with great happiness. He felt like singing, but noticed that old

Nephog Thoon was curled up asleep, and re-
frained.

It was difficult for him to believe that only seven
days had passed since he had escaped with Niane
from the doomed palace in the City of the Golden
Gates. So much had happened in so short a time,
so many world-shaking events had taken place,
that it seemed more like a month. An Empire had
fallen, a capital had been conquered, a dynasty
had collapsed, and they had fled halfway across the
island continent of Atlantis, through mountains,
above plains and forests, across the jungle coun-
tries, and now they sailed downriver for the safe
haven of Caiphul where they would join with the
White Emperor and deliver into his hands the
mighty Thing they had guarded through so many
perils. And not the least of these world-shaking
events was the amazing and wondrous love that
had flowered between the lovely young girl and
himself. He leaned on the pole, dreaming of a
happy future.

It was then the arrow took him in the shoulder
and he staggered backward off the raft and fell
into the rushing river.

Water closed over his head, filling his open
mouth, blinding his eyes. He sank like a stone,
weighed down by the heavy sword at his thigh.
Instinctively, he struck out with his hands but
white-hot agony lanced through his left shoulder
where the tufted arrow protruded. He opened his
mouth to voice an involuntary cry of pain, and
water rushed in, black water, closing about him,

pulling him down, smothering him. Then: nothing but darkness and coldness and pain, until these sensations dulled and went away and there was only darkness.

Nephog Thoon climbed to his feet unsteadily amidst a whooping of war cries and the flicker and thunk of arrows striking the raft. Niane shrieked as a feathered shaft pinned a fold of her gown to the rough wood of the raft. Diodric had fallen into the river. Kashonga, dozing, had snapped awake—warned by some primal sense of danger—and had plunged in after him.

All was noise and confusion. Dazed, the old sorcerer looked ahead. Both sides of the river were crowded with Dragon warriors. Arrows flickered through the hot, reeking air, sounding the distance. Shortly they would run a gamut of archers. For a moment, the old Lemurian wondered how the foemen—thought to be struggling along in their wake—had so magically appeared *ahead* of them. It seemed uncanny—miraculous! Then he remembered that doubling-back of the river only a short time before. The warriors of Gryphax must have rafted downstream, then crossed the narrow peninsula overland, landing ahead of the fleeing raft, in time to lay an ambush. But there was no time to think now.

He thrust forth his Staff and cried aloud a mighty Name. The sky darkened and the air grew still. Tension gathered, then broke in a thunderclap. A billow of black smoke exploded from the opposite shore. Bodies fell splashing in the shallows, or writhed in the mud, screaming, slapping at sparks.

The sorcerer hurled another bolt. It struck the mud of the nearer shore and detonated with an earth-shaking slap of sound. Black liquid mud heaved up, splattering the warriors clustered among tall reeds, drenching them, soaking their bows and blinding their eyes.

With a little grunt of satisfaction, he aimed yet another bolt—but a tall bearded figure on the shore was holding out a dark baton of glittering metal. Across the wide gap their eyes met, and Nephog Thoon knew that this was Gryphax, their implacable enemy. And he knew the thing in his hands. And fear entered into the soul of Nephog Thoon. He would have halted the bolt, but already it was sped. He felt, with senses other than the human, the wall of dark negation that flowed from the Blasting Wand Gryphax held. He knew what would happen when the two opposed forces met—he saw the sudden blaze of apprehension in the cold eyes of his adversary—but it was too late to do anything.

Then the world blew up. The impact hurled him into the water, which lifted in a towering fountain high into the sunlit sky. The raft exploded. He caught one swift glimpse of the girl amidst boiling waters, only the swirl of her loose black hair visible. Then the wave broke and drove him under into darkness.

And there was nothing else for a very long time.

★ 6 ★

The Book of Athothmose

The White Emperor, driven north-
wards, re-established himself in a city
on the southern edge of the mountainous district, which was now the seat of
one of the tributary kings. He gladly
welcomed the White Emperor and
placed the city at his disposal. A few
more of the tributary kings also remained loyal to him, but these did not
long remain faithful. Constant asser-
tions of independence were made by
the tributary kings, and continual battles were fought in different parts of
the Empire.

The sorcerers used their powers more
and more recklessly, and greater and
greater numbers of people practised
the terrible Black Arts.

Then came the awful retribution
when millions perished . . .

—W. SCOTT-ELLIOT: *Atlantis and
the Lost Lemuria* (edition of
1954, pp. 29–30)

i. The Gates of Caiphul

Cleon, Lord of the Empire and Captain-General of the West, had taken two days to cross the plains to the edges of the jungle country. He had gone forth at the bidding of the Great Seer of Atlantis, whose servants had rousted him from his bed on the evening of the seventh day after the fall of the distant capital. Although all of the city was deep in mourning and the sacred law was observed —no fires could be lit, no wine drunk, no man could enter into bed with wife or slave woman— he had been commanded to muster a strong force and ride out to succor those whom the Great Seer assured him he would find at the end of his journey.

He did not know what to expect, or whom he would encounter. The young priest who rode at his side in the chariot obviously knew, but would not tell. This youth, Sapherion, was tense and un-communicative: he stared straight ahead, white-faced, and seemed to begrudge every moment they were not riding forth across the plain. But Lord Cleon dourly insisted on rest stops. War birds and mortal men must sleep, he said harshly, even if priests did not.

They came to the green wall of the jungle, and skirted its edges for several hours, coming at last to the river. There the priest clutched his arm in a fierce grip, pointing without words. Cleon looked and saw a bedraggled party of muddy and half-naked scarecrows. There was an old man with his arm in a sling and an exhausted girl leaning on his other arm, and a huge Rmoahal savage dragging a fourth person on a litter. These people stopped short as the chariots advanced upon them. The elderly man—Cleon could tell from his wrinkled yellow skin he was a Lemurian—stepped forth as if to defend his comrades, which was odd, since he carried no weapon, not even a staff. But when his weary black eyes took in the Sun emblem on the breast of the charioteers and on the guidon that snapped in the afternoon breeze, he relaxed. He sat down suddenly, as if his legs could carry him no farther. The girl slumped as well, falling to her knees, and Cleon could see that she was weeping . . . weeping hopelessly, great racking sobs tearing through her. The gruff old commander softened at the sight of their misery, although he did not understand. They had endured terrible privations, but there was about them the heartbroken gloom of some greater loss or failure he could not comprehend.

He halted his troops and sprang stiffly from the chariot, going up to the old Lemurian while the priest ran forward to tend to the weeping girl.

The old man looked up at him blearily as Cleon approached. The old fellow was virtually skin and bones. He looked half starved and completely drained of strength.

"From Caiphul?" the old man croaked. Cleon nodded, unbuckling a canteen of fresh water from his belt and offering it silently. The old Lemurian's hands shook so badly he had to help him drink. He drank for a long time and finally put the bottle aside with a faint, weary nod of thanks. Cleon helped him to his feet.

"Is the Emperor in Caiphul?" the old man asked.

Cleon bowed his head grimly.

"The Divine One is dead," he said flatly. The other stared at him with wide eyes.

"Dead?" he repeated faintly. Cleon nodded somberly.

"The Divine Pnomphis was injured in his escape from the capital. One of the poisoned arrows of the Dragon. He died halfway to the haven of Caiphul and was buried along the way, such was the advance of the corruption caused by the filthy venom." Cleon spat, and shook his head, rubbing his brow.

Nephog Thoon stared off across the whispering grasses with a vague expression. He repeated the word *dead!* several times, as if he had forgotten the meaning of the word.

"But almost in the same hour, the Royal Lady was delivered of her babe. A son. Ere he fell into the last sleep, the Divine Pnomphis named his heir with the name Memthon. They spent but a brief while in Caiphul; then the Queen and the young Prince, together with what is left of the court, fled into hiding. Some say they have ventured over sea, to Tarshish in the Gadieric Land, as guests of King Arganthonios. Others say they journeyed further west to Trysadon or another city. We are not sure: wars have broken out in the south and west, between rival princes each claiming the Throne because of their descent from the Divine Atlas . . ."

"Madness, madness," the old man said hoarsely. "Each of the ten kings of Atlantis is descended from the Divine Atlas! Why do they not league together and overthrow the vile usurper who squats like a great toad, defiling the sacred Throne with his blasphemous touch?"

Wordlessly, Cleon shook his head. His aides were coming up to them now, with wine and food and medicinals, to tend to the exhausted wayfarers. He left the mumbling old man to their tender services, and turned to observe the rest of the party.

The young priest, Sapherion, had bathed the girl's gaunt face with a damp cloth and given her water and wine. He had been whispering urgently to her, and now, at Cleon's approach, he lifted a face white and strained and his voice was filled with despair as he cried: "Gone! Gone! *They have lost it!*"

Cleon did not know what Sapherion was talking about, but he could feel the urgency and the horror in the young priest's voice. Before he could do more than open his mouth to ask a question, he felt a touch on his arm and turned to see the mighty Rmoahal standing patiently by.

"What is it?" Cleon demanded.

The blue-skinned savage touched his hairless brow in respectful salute, and gestured with one muscular arm at the young man on the litter.

"Please, lord," the savage said simply. Cleon strode over to look at the boy who lay, tossing feebly, muttering under his breath, strapped to the crude litter. He looked once, then, slightly sickened, turned his face away.

"The arm will have to come off," he said gruffly. He had seen the results of the venomed arrows of the Dragon before.

"Oh—*no!*" a frightened voice cried sharply. The girl—she was skin and bones, clad in the filthy tatters of a gown—staggered over to clutch his arm and raise beseeching eyes to him. Eyes wide and haunted and huge in her wasted face. "Not his *arm!*" she cried. He patted her bony shoulder with a clumsy hand.

"There, there, lass. The arm *must* come off—it will poison the whole body, else. It is black and swollen."

She burst into a tempest of sobs and the young priest, still white and shaken by knowledge of the loss of the Thing he had come to take charge of, supported her frail body with his arms. He bent a thoughtful gaze on the feverish, tossing boy in the litter.

Then, giving the girl into the hands of one of the soldiers standing by, the young priest knelt and examined the injured youth. He touched his brow, laid the palm of his hand over the boy's heart, and seemed to be listening for something inaudible to the others. He turned swiftly to Cleon.

"Perhaps not," he said. "A Temple healer . . . we must get him to the city with all speed. Where are my medicines?"

For a time he worked over the youth. Then he rose, closing his pack, gesturing to a squadron of warriors standing near.

"You men! Take the Lord Diodric Asterion from the litter and into one of the pack chariots —tenderly, now."

Cleon's face paled and his eyes widened. The stab of awe went through him. He turned to look at the worn, empty faces of the half-starved travelers. *Diodric Asterion!* he thought hollowly, the beginnings of a vast amazement rising within him. *No wonder the Great Seer Athothmose commanded me to hurry? Gods of Atlantis, can THAT be the Thing they have lost?*

They took the exhausted wayfarers aboard the chariots and turned about with all speed, for the gates of Caiphul. With speed, with luck, with the favor of the Gods, they could get the young

Guardian of The Black Star into the hands of the great healers before the poison spread throughout his body.

Cleon grimly resolved to try.

This time there would be no rest stops.

ii. The Lost Hallow

It was three days later. Rested, clean, well fed, Niane and old Nephog Thoon recovered most of their exhausted strength. They were given a suite in the palace of the King of Caiphul. Strictly speaking, there was no king, for the late monarch had died battling for the Empire against the Dragon and the title was still being disputed among half a dozen claimants. Cleon, as Captain-General of the Empire in the West, held the city in his iron hand, and left it to the priesthood to figure out which of the six lordlings of Caiphul should mount the Royal Chair.

Niane's apartment was cool and dim and spacious. It opened on flowering gardens where little paths of white tiles wandered amid dewy grass and marble fountains splashed and danced in the clear sun. She slept for a day and a night, and awoke rested and refreshed. The priest-physicians of the Temple had tended to her bodily needs and she was whole again. Good food and more rest would repair the ravages of their long trek through the trackless jungle.

It had been a horrible ordeal, but it was over and she found to her surprise that she remembered but little of it. Kashonga had dragged her from the water after the two magical bolts had exploded, shaking the earth and drowning or blasting down all but a few of the Dragon warriors. She still could not understand how they had lived through that detonation of terrific power. Only the kindness of Heaven could account for it, she thought dimly.

Through it all the silent Kashonga had been a fortress of strength. He had dragged Diodric half-drowned from the river and pumped the water from his lungs and cut the arrow from his flesh. But the youth had not recovered consciousness: the venom on the barb raced through his veins and there was naught they could do to succor him. Poor old Nephog Thoon, his Staff of Power broken, his magical energy completely drained away, was like one in a daze. He tried, but he was of little help. Something he knew of herbs, and doubtless his physicking had helped hold back the advance of the poison in the boy's horribly swollen and blackening arm; but the old sorcerer was dull and vacant-eyed, and his wits wandered. He seemed to have lost all his strength, his courage, his intelligence. He stumbled along in their wake, mumbling vaguely to himself. He had taken no wound, she knew, but the backlash of the magical explosion had wrought terrible hurt to the old man. He might never fully recover his former mastery.

The Dragon warriors were all slain, driven mad, or fled. They found the half-eaten corpse of Gryphax where some jungle beast had dragged it. But they no longer cared. With Kashonga to guide them, burdened as he was with the feverish young Celt, they went through the jungle on foot for two days and two nights. There was no food, save for a few nuts and some rotten fruit which gave them the vomiting sickness. All game had fled the vicinity, their keen senses detecting the explosion of magic force. There was no meat. No meat. And no rest; for every hour lost brought the horribly injured youth that much closer to a degraded and loathsome death. So they had struggled forward on foot hour after hour, day after day, long past the limits of their strength. The explosion had drained them, as well, of vital force. They were very near death when the force from Caiphul had found them at last.

Perhaps the most terrible blow of all was the loss of The Black Star.

In the dull mood that had come upon their exhausted minds, none could recall just when it first occurred to them to search. Niane had a dim memory, however. At one point when Diodric was burning up with fever and his ravings had become hysterical, it seemed to her that the Gods might take pity on his agony if The Star was laid upon his naked breast. So she faintly remembered opening his ragged tunic and finding The Star was gone. Then things had dimmed for a time; somewhat later, she had apprised Nephog Thoon of her terrible discovery, and with hands that shook with unbelieving horror they had searched the boy's few garments and their own. They could not recall when they had last seen The Star. Had it not been in the glade when the saber-tooth had first attacked them? Why had they not made certain Diodric still had The Star on his person when Kashonga had helped him out of the pit, or, later, when they had again met with Nephog Thoon at the river's edge?

It had never occurred to them. The Star had simply faded from their minds during that long stretch of time. It was strange. It was frightening. As if some unseen Power had interfered with their memory.

What had happened to The Star? Had Diodric lost it when he fled from the tiger? Or had he lost it when he battled against Fang-Mouth in the pit? Or during the trek through the burning jungle— or the labor to build the raft, when he had tossed his tunic aside—or when the arrow had taken him in the shoulder and he had fallen into the river?

They did not know. They could not remember. But they only knew that The Black Star was lost to the knowledge of men.

Stretched on her couch in the languid afternoon stillness of old Caiphul, the girl Niane pressed her slim hands against her mouth and sobbed: "O Lord Rhamsheth Asterion, forgive me! I did my best. I did my very best . . ."

iii. In the Halls of Healing

When they were somewhat recovered from their
ordeal, Niane, Nephog Thoon, and Kashonga,
went to the Halls of Healing to visit Diodric. The
young priest Sapherion was their guide. He led
them through the whispering vastness of the great
Temple where dreaming faces of marble stood
among the shadows. The odor of nard and myrrh
drifted on the dim air. All was peace in the cool
shadows of the great Temple. A blessed and restful
hush of serenity ruled herein, and the clamor of
opposed and warring kingdoms was shut away outside when they left the open sun of the street.

Here was only Timelessness.

They had seen much of the priest Sapherion
in the last few days. He had tended to their wants
and spoken quietly with them. His superiors had
delegated to him the task of learning every detail
surrounding the loss of The Black Star, and this
he did with the utmost tact and delicacy. He
spoke to them with great deference in his voice
and manner. No man accused them of the loss, he
said quietly. All in Caiphul regarded them with
respect that bordered almost on veneration, for
they were the saviors of the most Sacred Thing in
Atlantis.

When Niane protested feebly that the Great Hallow had been lost through their carelessness and inattention, he refused to agree.

"Even if that were true, which it is not," he said gently, "no man can blame you for the accident. Had it not been for your great courage, the great courage and devotion of you all, the Dragon would have taken The Star into his clutch and everything would be lost. As it is, lacking The Star, his reign cannot long endure and he will go down into the Kingdom of Darkness and all his conquests and triumphs will have been in vain."

"But it is because of us that The Star was lost!" she said.

He smiled with great calm.

"Better a thousand times that the Great Treasure be lost, than that it fall into the hands of the Enemy," he said softly. "You and your friends endured great hardships and agony of body, mind and soul, in the defense of the Holiness. Where all others forgot, or failed, or fled, you remained steadfast. You are *Niane Asterion,* I say, and your name will not be forgotten on the lips of men."

He smiled, and turned to the silent Rmoahal who strode beside them. "You too, my huge friend! You are Kashonga Asterion, and the Gods will love you for your faithful service to your friends."

Kashonga grunted and nodded with great dignity. He knew nothing of stars, or of the Atlantean Gods.

Friendship was the name of that which he worshiped.

They had lain Diodric upon a soft couch in the
Hall of the Great Seer. For a day and a night had
he lain there in the presence of the Ancient One,
after he had come from the gentle hands of the
healer-priests, who could do no more for his body.

The poison had been drained and the power of
the healers had repaired much of the ravagement
of his weak flesh. But his mind—his soul—had
wandered far along dark grim paths—almost to the
shadowy gates of the Kingdom of Darkness. He
could not, alone, retrace that far journeying.

As they came into the hall, none of them saw
the figure on the throne. All they could see was the
white wasted face of Diodric. He lay in deep restful slumber, and his face was turned toward the
figure on the throne as the face of a flower turns
toward the sun from whence cometh its life.

It was terribly wasted, that young face. The
cheeks were sunken in. The temples were hollowed.
Great dark rings lay under the eyes. But the lips
were smiling faintly and the bloom of health was
upon his pallid flesh. His chest rose and fell with
deep breathing. His ribs were plainly visible under the light coverlet. But Niane could see only
one thing, and her eyes filled with tears and her
heart with joy as she saw it.

They had not taken off his arm.

Pale and scrawny, but whole, it lay motionless
on the coverlet.

She knelt, a sob of happiness gathering in her throat, and lay her cheek softly against his hand and kissed it.

A quiet gentle voice sounded from behind her.

"He heals, daughter, but slowly. The Gods willing, all will yet be well with him."

They turned to see the man upon the throne. He was very old. His hair was like white silk. His beard fell like a snowy banner to his lap. His flesh was like wax. All they could see in his pale lean face were the great deep eyes. They were dark, those eyes, and gentle: much wisdom was in them, and they had looked upon many long years of time, far more years than are given to other men, but they were not weary, those eyes, of looking. Youth was in them, the unquenchable spark of the joy of life. They laughed sweetly, those dark eyes. They were as fresh and innocent and joyful as the eyes of a boy.

From his snowy robes and golden cap they knew him for the Great Seer, and they knelt respectfully. He lifted one thin transparent hand, beckoning them nearer.

"My daughter, I have been with him in the far places and in the empty wastes. I guide him back to the Land of the Living, to which no man so wandered hence can return without a guide."

"Lord—*will* he recover?" she asked tremulously.

"He will live to sire strong sons to fight for Prince Memthon when he enters his kingdom again, yea, and those sons will seek the lost Star all the days of their lives, for the glory of that task

the Gods will set upon them—not in retribution
for any fault or sin of you twain, my child, but in
honor of the greatness of your courage and of your
suffering in the cause of The Lost Hallows."

She bowed her head to hide the tears.

"Oh Lord Athothmose, Holy Father, will The
Star be found again?" she whispered. He nodded
slowly, the snowy beard and long white hair catching fire from a vagrant sunbeam until there was a
blaze of glory about his beautiful ancient face like
the halo of the saints.

"The Black Star will be found again in the full-
ness of time and when the peoples of Atlantis are
strong and sure in the Cause of Light," he said.
"But this will not come in my time, nor in yours.
Mayhap in the day of your sons, or of your son's
sons, but this I cannot say."

The young priest Sapherion who knelt beside
them addressed the ancient Sage in tones of great
respect.

"Great One, we have gathered from these poor
people every detail surrounding the loss of The
Holy. We are ready to begin the quest. A hundred
priests, nobles and warriors have sworn the Oath
of Brotherhood as was your decree."

The old patriarch nodded with gentle dignity.

"Let it begin, then," he said slowly.

Niane cried: "Holy Father, when we are well
and hardy again—may we join this Brotherhood?"

"You may join in the Brotherhood of The
Black Star, my child," he said slowly, "but not
in the Quest of The Star. You have done much in

the cause; now is time to rest a little, to wed, to find new lives for yourselves. Let others take up the search: it is your turn to live. Now go, for I have much to do. But return tomorrow at this hour, and mayhap the one you love will be awake from his long slumbering."

They left the presence of the Great Seer of Atlantis with joy and thankfulness in their hearts.

iv. The Long Night

There came wars and the rumors of wars to south and to west. Great hosts were abroad and battles fought and kings disthroned, until none could truly say that this man ruled, or that man, or yet another. But through this all, Caiphul weathered the storm, for it was far from the centers of habitation, and surrounded by the green wall of the jungle and the black wall of the mountains. The people held their guard and the priests offered sacrifice, and the city remained faithful to Memthon the True Emperor, and there was peace in that land. Perhaps it was due to the legend of the great weapons which men whispered lay ready to hand in the ancient crypts of Caiphul. Or possibly the presence of Four Asteria within the walls placed all of the city under the guardianship of Heaven. For whatever the cause, war came not to trouble Caiphul, though all the land else was racked with torment until thousands lay dead and rotting.

Of all this, Diodric knew but little. He lay lapped in peace, his body knitting slowly, and his mind nurtured to health again by the blessed arts of the Great Seer, who was known among men as Athothmose, although the Immortal Gods knew Him by another name, of which I may not speak.

In time he could rise from his couch and walk in the gardens. Niane was most often with him and they talked of their future together, and of the new life they would build here in Caiphul, which had opened its arms to the great heroes who had saved The Star from falling into the hands of the servants of Chaos.

But of The Black Star they did not speak.

It was a month almost to the day after they had first entered into the gates of Caiphul that they were wed in the Great Temple, with all the lords of Caiphul in attendance, and the new King himself there to bless their union. It was a great day. The city was decked as if for festival; flags flew and there were flowers everywhere, and smiling happy faces. The Brotherhood of a hundred had grown, by this time, to number a thousand. The two newlyweds went forth from the Temple under an avenue of arched swords held aloft by the thousand questers of The Star. They went forth in a thunder of golden trumpets into the open sun. The maidens of Caiphul scattered flowers under their feet and a thousand snow-white pigeons were set loose from the tower windows to fill the skies with white wings. Laughing, blushing, Niane hung on his arm and he could feel the beating of her heart against his arm.

And Diodric felt very much married.

There came a time when earth, sea, and sky were troubled. The sky went dark at midday, and the earth shuddered underfoot like a frightened thing, and the sea darkened to the color of oiled metal. War birds fought in the pens; mammoths trumpeted their terror from the plains; and flocks of birds were seen flying from the shores of Atlantis, as if seeking a haven somewhere in the empty and desolate seas.

Men said that the Gods were angry at the abominations of the black magicians who ruled yet at the City of the Golden Gates. In truth, the sorcerers of Chaos had gone beyond all previous limits in their use of the Forbidden Arts. Three armies had they crushed with their terrible magic, and whole provinces were laid waste. Plague and famine hovered over Atlantis, and such prodigies of blasphemous sorcery were worked by the Priests of Chaos that it seemed the very earth itself shrank from the feet of the Dragon warriors in shuddering revulsion.

Came then a day and a night of terror when the earth trembled and stars shot madly from their spheres to streak the unnatural darkness of the troubled skies with tears of phosphoric flame.

And heralds came riding in haste from the King

to rouse Diodric and Niane and their other companions from their beds in the middle of the night. Chariots clattered through the streets and men shouted from the rooftops and none knew if the world was coming to an end or if all of Atlantis was sinking to its doom beneath the heaving waves.

The Asteria were brought with all haste into the great hall of the Temple. A thousand priests and lords and warriors stood about, or knelt, and all were listening with awe and terror to the tired whispering voice that spoke from the mighty throne. Athothmose was far from his body this night, his soul had gone winging into the vast unknown over leagues of night-enshrouded land, to view the terrible cataclysm that shook the City of the Golden Gates in this terrible hour.

They knelt near his throne, staring up, listening with wonder and with horror to his slow words.

"... Falling! Falling! Oh, the towers falling! The streets are filled with people. I see their white faces staring up like a field of white flowers. O the pity of it—the pity! The babes, the children ..."

"What is he talking about?" Diodric demanded of the old noble who knelt next to them.

"The vengeance of the Gods hath fallen upon Black Thelatha," the old man said.

"The Sea is coming now ... the Sea! Like a mountain of waters, moving ... they see the mighty wave and they cry out, imploring Heaven, but Heaven will not hear ... the Sea comes in ... the docks in the harbor give way like matchwood un-

*der the sprawling weight of the Sea . . . the faces
are swept away . . . the Sea moves through the
streets and the palaces and the great temples fall,
one by one . . ."*

"Pazadon, Rhakotis, Polinax, and All Gods!"
gasped the young Celtic warrior; "It is the end of
the world!"

"It is the end of *Thelatha*," said Nephog
Thoon with grim satisfaction in his harsh voice.
But the entranced Seer was speaking again faintly.
His transparent lids were closed over his staring
eyes, his waxen hands strove feebly with empty air
as if to beat away the terrible vision he saw with
his Inward Eye. Now his distraught voice became audible again.

"*. . . Up to the Mount, the Sacred Mount, sweep
the great waves . . . the walls of the Great House
give way . . . a thousand tons of water thunder
down upon the Black Throne where Thelatha the
Accursed sits dead as stone, smitten with the
lightning of the Gods! Ah, his priests strive to drag
his corpse from the place of power . . . they would
bury him in the great Necropolis, in a secret
tomb . . . but all are crushed beneath the waves
. . . All? Do any live to take him from the broken
chair? I cannot see, I cannot see . . .*"

The voice died away in a shrill wailing, and
there was silence for a time. The earth shuddered
a little underfoot, and thunder growled in the
bowels of Heaven. Men and women knelt, their
faces turned away or hidden in their hands, and
none there was that dared to look his neighbor in

the eye in this dread and terrible hour.

And suddenly all were electrified as a great, echoing cry of horror and despair went thundering up from the writhing, white-faced figure on the high throne. There was a world of sorrow and agony in that despairing cry, and a world of pity.

And a world was ending in that sobbing cry from the high throne:

"Alas . . . alas . . . alas! Alas, that great City, that great City . . . that is fallen and shalt rise no more . . ." sobbed the Lord Athothmose the Great Seer of Atlantis.

v. The Sorcerer Comes Home

Half a year later, a bent shuffling figure went toiling through the foothills of the Mountains of the Terror. The sky was overcast and evening was nearly come. Thunder grumbled among the hills. Up the dusty road he came, bent and hunched and leaning on a plain staff of old wood, a knapsack thrown over his back. With luck he would reach home before the rains came.

He had trudged far, the old man, and he was tired. Tired of the world and its ways and wars, and anxious to stretch out in comfort before the fires of his own hearth, sipping a mug of ripe brown ale, able to rest his weary legs at last.

It was just as he had left it, the tall tower of dark smooth stone that rose on the crest of the wooded hill. The curious green roses grew still over the ancient doorway, and turned stiffly to observe him as he came shuffling up to the threshold.

His magical garden had run wild and rank with weeds, he saw. Doubtless a whole crop of mandrake roots had been lost. Well, well, as for that—more and better things had been lost than a batch of squeaking, viper-eyed mandrakes! Aye, and more and better things found as well, he thought, with a fond smile, thinking of Diodric and Niane and silent Kashonga who had become their friend and companion, their servant and guardian, and who would not leave them for his jungle home.

"I'm home, Szaliel!" he called, as the door opened before its master. "Draw my bath hot, and set a fire on the grate, and fetch me mulled ale in my earthenware cup."

So Nephog Thoon came home at the end of his journey.

Thunder grumbled and the gale whooped and bellowed about the mullioned windows. Rain lashed the walls of old stone. It was a filthy night. But the weary old sorcerer did not care.

He stretched out in his great chair, toasting his toes before the fire, wrapped in a warm, snuff-colored robe, a stocking cap pulled down to his ears to guard his bald old pate against the night damps and chills. He had feasted sumptuously on roast beef and boiled carrots and liver and kidney pie, washed down with copious draughts of good ale, and now he rested, soaking up the warmth, a comfortable feeling of repletion radiating from his middle.

He sipped his mug, staring with dreamy, thoughtful eyes into the flickering heart of the flames. Then he absently dipped his hand into the knapsack that lay slumped beside the chair. He drew out something, a small flat box of orichalc, opened it, and took forth a glittering dark Thing.

The glory of The Black Star outshone the flames.

Staring at it, blinking against its splendor, his old eyes became misted with tears. His lips moved soundlessly. Then:

"Forgive me! . . . my young friends, forgive me! It was not I who would do the thing, but others bade me do it . . ." A tear ran down his wrinkled yellow cheek and he wiped it away with the back of one bony old hand.

"I have betrayed you, and you know it not," he sniffed.

"You have betrayed no one at all, elder brother," a voice said from the shadows behind him. Nephog Thoon did not have to turn around to know the tall figure standing there in hooded robes of gray, a quiet smile on his smooth, youngish face.

"Come here, Kynaethon, you scoundrel! Take a seat before the fire so I can look at you. I am too old to play guessing-games amid the shadows."

The younger Thaumaturgist smilingly obeyed,

and sat across from him on a low stool. He extended one hand, took The Star and its orichalcum box and looked deep within the precious Thing. Its dancing fires painted glory on his face and set the spark of mystery in his eyes. He looked long upon It.

"It is very beautiful," he sighed.

"It is that, and more," said Nephog Thoon grumpily.

He watched the other place the Jewel within its box and slip the box within a pocket of his robes.

"It was needful that I do the deed, I suppose," the old Lemurian grumbled.

"It was very needful," said Brother Kynaethon gently.

"Even at the cost of betraying them?" demanded the sorcerer.

"Even at such a price," Kynaethon said.

Nephog Thoon noisily drained his great mug, and set it down in empty air. It snapped out of existence. He folded his bony old hands across his plump middle and heaved a gusty sigh. But he said nothing; he stared broodingly into the dancing flames. He blinked sleepily.

"The Black Star must go into hiding for an age," said Kynaethon softly, after a time. "The Lords of Life have thus decreed. None may know of this. Not even the priests of the Gods. Not even the Great Seer himself, although I think the Lord Athothmose suspects something of the truth. If so, no matter. The Thaumaturgae shall keep the Hallow safe until an age is done."

"Will The Star ever be found?" inquired the Lemurian gloomily.

The younger man nodded. "Of course! But not in our time. Much evil must pass from the Sacred Land. Men must find within themselves the strength and the courage to endure the Long Night that is now upon them. A thousand men shall search for a thousand years. Men of nobility and honor and self-sacrifice. In the end, one of them will reap undying glory. For unto him it shall be given to fulfill the quest. The Black Star will not be hidden forever. But it must be hidden for a time."

The old man sighed and wiped his eyes.

"Alas, for young Diodric! How it pained me to filch the Thing from his sleeping body, the dear lad! But he fell to sleep and the others with him, by my spell. They had no choice—but it was not fair! They thought me their friend, their comrade."

Strange fires shone within the eyes of Kynaethon of the Thaumaturgae.

"Do not mourn for the Lord Diodric Asterion," he said in a great voice. "For he is no dupe, no pawn, but hath a great part to play in a mighty Plan. And it shall be a son of his line who shall find The Black Star, at the end of the age. Aye, and a destiny greater even than that is being planned for him! This I swear unto you, elder brother!"

Nephog Thoon eyed him sourly, mouth pursed in distaste.

"You take much upon yourself," he observed.

The younger man was suddenly humble. He shook his head.

"I am the lowest of the low," he confessed. "I am but a servant of Those far greater than you or I. I am nothing."

Nephog Thoon cleared his throat as if making an assent. And suddenly he was alone. The young Thaumaturgist was gone, and The Star gone with him.

"Hmmph!" grunted Nephog Thoon. Then he yawned a great jaw-cracking yawn. It was time for bed and he was very weary.

We shall leave him there, cozy and warm in his great chair, thinking of the great deeds he had seen and the high adventures in which he had played a part, aye, and not the smallest of roles, either.

Outside the old stone tower, the storm bellowed and lightning blazed. The Long Night had come down over the Sacred Land. And no man then alive would live to see the coming of the Dawn.

*

The Sequel to This Novel Will Be Known as
THE WHITE THRONE

The Epilogue to *The Black Star*

It is written:

The great City of the Golden Gates had by this time become a perfect den of iniquity.

The waves swept over it and destroyed its inhabitants, and the Black Emperor and his dynasty fell to rise no more.

The continent was now terribly rent. But the actual amount of territory submerged by no means represented the damage done, for tidal waves swept over great tracts of land and left them desolate swamps. Whole provinces were rendered barren, and remained for generations in an uncultivated and desert condition.

The remaining population too had received a terrible warning. It was taken to heart, and sorcery was for a time less prevalent among them.

A long period elapsed before any new powerful rule was established.

—W. Scott-Elliot: *Atlantis and the Lost Lemuria* (edition of 1954, p. 30)

The Notes to *The Black Star*

Let me make it plain that this is a work of imaginative fiction, written with no higher motive than merely to entertain its readers with what I hope is a colorful and exciting novel of fantastic adventures. I do not pretend to set forth herein, under the guise of fiction, any serious theories of prehistory; neither do I pretend to familiarity with any occult lore or secret records forbidden to the general run of humanity.

However, it is true that much of the settings and scenery of this novel derive from a close study of Classical authorities and a rather comprehensive knowledge of the occult literature that has been written on the subject of Atlantis. It has occurred to me that a few of my readers might enjoy knowing something of the sources from which this "factual" data has been mined: hence these

Notes, which any reader not of scholarly inclinations can safely skip.

Incidentally, there are certain questions raised in *The Black Star* that are left unanswered. This is not, I hope, due to any carelessness on my part, but to the fact that this novel is intended as the first volume of an Atlantis Trilogy.

—LIN CARTER

The Notes:

1. As to the personal and place names used herein, some are of my own coinage and others are derived from various sources. The name "Atlantis" itself comes, of course, from the two Atlantean dialogues of Plato (born about 427 B.C.), a disciple of Socrates and himself one of the greatest of the ancient Greek philosophers, whose teachings and inquiries have continued to be a major influence on human thought for 2,400 years. It is not true, as often stated, that Plato calls the Atlantic island "Poseidonis." I have studied the two key dialogues, wherein the Atlantis story is given, in their original Greek texts, and Plato uses the name 'Ατλαντις (Atlantis) in the nominative case; Greek being an inflective language, the word-endings naturally vary when used in the dative or accusative case; he nowhere uses the name

"Poseidonis" for the island. If it bothers the reader that names like "Atlantis" and "Diodric," which sound if anything Greek, should coexist with names like "Pnomphis" and "Memthon," which sound more Egyptian than anything else, and both in the context of a civilization presumed to exist many thousands of years *before* either Greece or Egypt, you may be amused to discover that the same detail also bothered Plato. In the second of his Atlantean dialogues, the *Critias,* he carefully points out: "You must not be surprised at often hearing me mention Grecian names of barbarous men. For the cause of this is as follows: Solon intending to insert this narration into his verses, investigated for this purpose the power of names, and found that those first Egyptians who committed these particulars to writing transferred these names into their own tongue." In other words, the Egyptian records from which, according to Plato, his ancestor Solon first heard the Atlantis story, had "Egyptianized" place and personal names from the original Atlantean language; Plato goes on to admit that Solon, upon learning this, promptly "Greekized" the Egyptian names for *his* account. Hence we have not the slightest idea of what the Atlanteans themselves called their island (if there ever *were* any Atlanteans), and can do nothing but repeat names like "Atlas" from the Platonic dialogues.

2. (Part 1, Chap. vi.) That the Atlanteans used some form of aircraft is frequently mentioned in the occult sources. Scott-Elliot (p. 52) says: "The

material of which the air boats were constructed was either wood or metal . . . in shape they were boatlike, but decked over, for when at full speed it could not have been convenient to remain on the upper deck. Their propelling and steering gear could be brought into use at either end." I have assumed, for my story, that the *viwân* was invented by the Lemurians. W. S. Cerve (in *Lemuria: The Lost Continent in the Pacific,* p. 89) says: "Lemuria itself was continuing to sink in the western portion, forcing all of the people to move to parts of Asia. . . . The continent of Atlantis had become peopled with pilgrims and colonists from Lemuria;" and, in reference to the *viwân,* he says (p. 170): "I have spoken of how they (i.e. the Lemurians) were able to propel their boats in water by using the energy that radiated from a stone. Undoubtedly a similar device was used in propelling their airships [which] were lighter and much different in design from anything we have been able to attain." All of these details appear in my novel. *Viwân* is the Sanskrit word the ancient Aryan epics, such as the *Purânas* or the *Ramayana,* use to refer to the flying vehicles which made up the immense aerial navies of the prehistoric civilizations they call *Sveta-Dwipa* and *Hiranya-Dwipa,* which according to Theosophical authorities are Atlantis and Lemuria respectively. Further information on the airboats can be found in my series of Lemurian novels about the barbarian hero, Thongor the Mighty: the background mythos of the Lemurian romances is obviously contiguous with that of this Atlantis Trilogy. As for Cerve's reference to "power from stones," the motive influence in the airboats, I call these power crystals *sithurls* (literally "sun-stones," from *Sithya,* the Lemurian name of the sun, and *turul,* the Lemurian word for "stone" in the sense of "gemstone" or "crystal"); in the Atlantis readings of Edward Cayce, the renowned American psychic, the power crystals are called *tuaoi.* They apparently absorbed solar energy, stored it, and transformed it into electricity.

3. (I, viii.) My description of the City of the Golden Gates is drawn from a careful study of Plato's description, which appears in the *Critias* and which contains a wealth of detail, even to the colors of stone used in the buildings, the ornamentation on the Temple of Poseidon which stood on the Sacred Mount, and the existence of a hippodrome. Plato, incidentally, does not use the name "City of the Golden Gates." I have borrowed the term from Theosophical writers such as Scott-Elliott, as it is by now well established in Atlantis fiction. Such terms as "The White Emperor" and "the Divine Dynasty," used herein, also come from Scott-Elliot. My references to the Ten Cities of Atlantis, however, come from Plato. As he does not give any of their names, I have taken some of the names of the cities used herein from other Classical writers who have discussed Atlantis (such as Diodorus Siculus, who preserves an account of the wars of Queen Myrine of Cherronesos against the Atlantean city of Kernë). My infor-

mation on the Lemurian dynasty and the golden age of Caiphul (which is scattered throughout *The Black Star,* but which appears particularly in IV, i) is partly conjectural and based on the two conflicting accounts of Atlantean kingship, that is, the settlement by Lemurian colonists and the story that Poseidon fathered the Divine Atlas on the nymph Cleito, thus founding the Empire (I have reconciled the conflicting accounts by presuming two successive Empires, the First or Lemurian, centered at Caiphul, and the Second or Atlantide, centered at the City of the Golden Gates), and partly drawn from a description of the advanced scientific civilization of the Atlanteans at Caiphul in the age of Zailm Numinos, which I have taken from a book called *A Dweller on Two Planets,* attributed to an Atlantean named Phylos. "Phylos," by the way, is hardly in any position to accuse me of literary theft, since he himself states in the most positive of terms that his book is not fiction but historical fact—and historical data, of course, can hardly be copyrighted by him or by anyone, since nobody invented it.

4. (I, viii.) The metal *kassiteros* is known to us as tin. As for *orichalcum* (sometimes called "orichalc" or "aurichalcum"), the mystery metal of the Atlanteans has yet to be identified. The word is more correctly spelled (by direct transliteration from the Greek) *oreichalkon:* from a study of the roots, it would seem to mean something like "mountain-bronze," but no one knows what that is supposed to mean. Plato describes it as if it were

a precious metal, like gold, silver or electrum; or, at very least, a *rare* metal, and hence valuable. At any rate, Plato did not invent the word; writers earlier than he use it (the poet Hesiod, for example). No metal known to us of today would seem to resemble it (Plato describes it as "flashing with red light" in *Critias;* oddly enough, he does not even mention the metal in *Timaeus*).

5. (III, i.) Some miscellaneous notes. Readers who may chance to be intrigued by my references to that very ancient text known as *The Lemurian Chronicles* will find more information, together with copious quotations from the text, in any of my Lemurian romances, such as *Thongor at the End of Time,* for example. I happen to possess the only complete copy of the *Chronicles* known to exist: this work of Elder Lore describes the Creation, the reign of the pre-human Hyperboreans, and the earliest of human civilizations down to the height of the Golden Empire of the Sun which ruled Lemuria.

As for Pazadon, the Atlantean sea divinity, his name is Atlantean in origin (from *Paz,* "sea, or ocean"; and *Adon,* "Lord"), and it survived into historical times as *Poseidon* among the Greeks. And, as for the City of the Sphinx, Sait-ya, in the Land of Khem-Mu, or Egypt: Sait-ya is the elder name of the city of the Nile delta known to the Greeks as Sais. The occult writers unanimously attribute the founding of Sais to the Atlanteans; therein certain Atlantean records are supposed to have survived the Cataclysm which destroyed the island continent. These records, whether in whole or merely in part is unknown, were engraven on two Pillars. Plato tells us that his source for the Atlantean narrative was a document written by Solon, and Plutarch informs us that Solon learned many things from Egyptian priests while he was at Sais, thus corroborating Plato's account of the origin of his data. The philosopher Crantor, who was the first known commentator on Plato's works, accepted the Atlantis story as genuine history and affirmed that the temple records from which Solon got the tale were still preserved at Sais in his day. And we have independent evidence of this from another writer, a historian named Theopompus of Chios who was one of Plato's contemporaries: Theopompus also visited Egypt, also studied the Sais records, and also recorded some historical information about Atlantis—information, by the way, which was *not* included in Plato's very cursory account of Atlantean history. Hence my references to "Sait-ya."

6. (IV, i.) As for the Atlantean elephants, we have the word of Plato, who says in *Critias:* "Whatever, too, the woods afford for builders the island produced in abundance. There were likewise sufficient pastures for tame and savage animals; together with a prodigious number of elephants." A glance at the evolutionary record of geologic time, the varieties of mastodon and mammoth native to Europe before, during and after the last Ice Age, and the approximate date in which the events in my novel presumably took place, combine to per-

suade me these "Atlantean elephants" were really
the great wooly mammoths and not the modern
African or Indian pachyderms.

7. (IV, iii.) Descriptions of the Lemurian *zamph*
and *kroter* can be found in any of my Lemurian
romances. As for the giant wingless bird, the steed
used by the Atlanteans in place of the horse, which
had yet to be introduced into Europe at this period, I have made a guess and called this species
the *garuda*. In the ancient Sanskrit epics, which
Madame Blavatsky and other occult authorities
presume to have preserved accounts of both Lemuria and Atlantis, there are frequent references
to the *garuda,* a bird used as a steed by various
of the Aryan heroes. I own a richly detailed sculp-
ture from Indonesia which depicts one of the
mythological heroes mounted on a *garuda,* which
I have used as the basis for my brief description.

8. (VI, iv.) My account of the destruction of the
City of the Golden Gates and the death of Thelatha the Demon King is conjecture based on the
occult literature. Scott-Elliot says the City of the
Golden Gates was destroyed in a deluge, and that
"the Black Emperor and his dynasty fell to rise no
more"; however this was many thousands of years
before the final Cataclysm itself. Atlantis, during
its long history, is believed to have suffered many
localized catastrophes, and even the final Cataclysm (the traditional date is 9,564 B.C.) did not
completely destroy the continent, for the small
isle of Poseidonis survived until a very late date.
Clark Ashton Smith has set his excellent tales of